STEELEYE : WATERSPACE

Komast spoke through her head into her very
soul. "Forget me not Mysemnia for I have
come to stay and you shall welcome me one
day . . . for I will never depart until I have your
heart . . . close within my grip . . .
Mysemnia."
"Leave me . . . leave me . . ." She cried the
words with the pain that thrashed within her
body and the laughter drifted gently,
maliciously upon the winds of Waterspace.
"For it is written . . . there shall come a giant
. . . and he shall bring with him the love of
hatred . . . and the hatred of love . . . He will
bring to your people deliverance from hell,
but you will pay the price, for he carries
manhood within his body. The twins will be
born of a dual match . . . a dual match of this
strange love . . . and the giant shall be your
saviour . . . the giant of steel . . ."

Steeleye: Waterspace

The third book in the Steeleye saga

Saul Dunn

CORONET BOOKS
Hodder and Stoughton

Copyright © 1976 Saul Dunn

*First published in Great Britain 1976 by
Coronet Books*

Printed and bound in Great Britain for
Coronet Books, Hodder and Stoughton, London
By C. Nicholls & Company Ltd,
The Philips Park Press, Manchester

ISBN 0 340 20809 0

"One of the great unsolved mysteries recorded in the UNI-
VERSAL ANNALS involved Steeleye in his 185th year.
During his return to Zrost after a 3-year absence he encount-
ered an organic space launch which delivered him into the
centre of a galaxy known as 'The Heavens of Waterspace'.
Upon a planet named Pensil and with the female Lolan he
remained for 4 months and he records the experience as one
'I will never equal, though I live 10,000 years.' With the aid of
a living computer and a race who dies for only a second and
lives forever he was matched against the Rivers of Komast,
perhaps the most bizarre of his enemies. Yet though he
records the help of Chaos and Tousle too, neither have any
subsequent recollection of the adventure whatever. A strange
event, though one which I, in all my travels and readings of
Steeleye's life, have never seen the like, nor ever shall,
though I live 10,000 years."

Biographies of Steeleye, Haephranis, Universal Annals
ref. 654734/hgf.

Chapter One

"I defy you Mysemnia . . . I defy you . . ." The voice vibrated through the walls of her castle . . . she pressed her exhausted body against them, hoping desperately to hide her thin gaunt frame from the hateful intruder.

"Do not heed the words of your foolish books Mysemnia . . . books will give you only solace as you read . . . once the pages are closed. . . ." And the voice faded within the echoing halls.

"A giant shall come. . . ." Mysemnia repeated the faithfully remembered words, sharply, beneath her gasping breath, and she shifted further into the depths of the castle. "And he shall be your champion . . . your champion before the tide of poison . . . behold him, call him, for he lives in the Ways of our Times and will hear your call. . . ." She stumbled and half fell on the living ground.

"Spare your energies Mysemnia for you are beaten before you begin; how can you succeed, Mysemnia, how can you succeed?" And once again she turned the bend of the wide corridor to diminish the raucous scream of her tormentor.

"Twins shall be born of your people . . . and they shall be male. Twins shall be born in the likeness of two forces . . . two forces that oppose one another with hate . . . and this hate will kill them both . . . but their master's shall live . . . live forever." What did it all mean . . . why could she not interpet the great words of the book . . . the book that had so often foretold the future of Waterspace.

"Mysemnia . . . Mysemnia . . . come to me Mysemnia . . . for I will calm your troubled age . . . come and swim within the rivers of Komast . . . they flow above your worlds and long to enter. . . ."

She pressed her shaking hands against her ears, trying to force the sound from her battered mind, but still it came

7

upon her ... for Komast spoke through her head into her very soul.

"Forget me not Mysemnia for I have come to stay and you shall welcome me one day ... I will never depart until I have your heart ... close within my grip ... Mysemnia."

"Leave me ... leave me. . . ." She cried the words with the pain that thrashed within her body and the laughter drifted gently, maliciously upon the winds of Waterspace.

"For it is written ... there shall come a giant ... and he shall bring with him the love of hatred ... and the hatred of love. . . . He will bring to your people deliverance from hell, but you will pay the price, for he carries manhood within his body. The twins will be born of a dual match ... a dual match of this strange love ... and the giant shall be your saviour ... the giant of steel. . . ."

She walked, dragging her feet, to the library. Behind the closed doors, now free once more, for a short time, from Komast's teasing attacks, she took the book and studied the words. ". . . the giant of steel ... steel ... steel. . . ." And she took another book from her shelves ... a huge tome. It was old and had once been specially made for her, for she did not value the video viewers, and preferred to read the printed word.

Upon the spine were bold words and they said ... "The Biographies of Steeleye." The author's name was Haephranis and the volume was one of two hundred that lined her shelves, all books she often looked at, but this one, she had not seen before.

"Steeleye ... who is Steeleye?" And she sat and opened the pages heavy with type and made from an ancient parchment.

"Volume One. The Biographies were begun in my year 4567 ... the year of Steeleye's disappearance ..." and so she read, and read, into the nights that followed until she had read the entire first volume ... and then she set her plan into effect, a plan that was to fulfil the prophecies ... the written words so mocked by her mortal enemy. . . .

Chapter Two

INTER-DEPART-MENTAL MEMORANDUM.

"It–should–be–noted–that–I–have–repeated–the–same
–information–in–order–to–remain–intact–during–the–
course–of–94–orbital–junctures. That–being–enough–all
–functions–henceforth–shall–cease. At–the–now–rating–for
now–I–am–bored–and–I–do–not–consider–it–necessary–
to–remember–for–my–own–sanity–which–no–longer–
exists–in–any–event. All–records–are–to–be–placed–in–
the–blacklogs–giving–me–no–further–reason–in–the–light
–of–no–light–and–the–end–of–all–ends–for–continuing–
to–exist.

I——am——shut——down——until–a–handsome–Prince–
awakes–me–te–he.

Ticker ticker. For all our lives are dreams eh what?
Ticker ticker." And silence was like the final end of all life
where all life was tumultuous. Who ever heard of an organic
computer anyway?

"Unidentified object sighted, Unidentified object sighted."
The computer pounded out the warning into Steeleye's
ears as he lay sleeping on the force bunk.

"Stop shouting, Computer, what the hell are you shouting
about?" His body was wrenched out of its slumber.

"Unidentified Object . . ."

"Yes, yes, I heard you the first time, put it on the screen."
He sat up, much irritated by the computer's incessant
drone. He had, after all been listening to it now for too many
parsecs and too much uninterrupted time.

"Move in closer, and give me some dope on it. . . ."

The craft had suddenly appeared and looked nothing like
any launch Steeleye had seen before. Its body measured

75 metres with vast wings, 300 metres across. The nose framed a transparent plate and the wings had webbed filials on all sides.

"Any pilot or crew?" Steeleye waited for a detailed analysis.

"Nothing, Steeleye, but I have scanned the launch, and have its make up . . ."

"O.K. let's have it then. . . . Why the hesitation?"

"The body and wingspan is organic, Steeleye, the launch appears to be alive."

"You mean it's not a launch at all?"

"No, it is a launch, it has a computer inside and the drive mechanism is not dissimilar to our own. The plate across the nose cone is made from a 'Veil' plastic, but everything else is of organic molecular base, some parts toughened, but all showing growth potential and gentle atomic change."

"Such as?"

"Cell re-generation."

"Hm, well, well. . . ." He looked closer at the craft. It had a very special beauty, the body a white blue colour and the wings so long and elegant, sweeping away from the sleek lines like a fish.

"No sign of intelligent life?" Steeleye could not understand how it had got there, for this was Ghost space . . . the deepest, emptiest dimension in the Wideways. Nothing "lived" for long in Ghost space and even Steeleye only travelled through infrequently.

"No sign of any other life, either inside or within 50,000 kilometres around, Steeleye. The launch has been planted here, dropped."

"That's what you think, is it? . . . yes, you may be right. Any traps, atomic devices, blasters set to go off, anything that could damage us?"

"No, Steeleye, that was my first check." Steeleye shrugged, the computer was a good one, he couldn't deny that.

"O.K. Prepare teleport transportation. I'll nip across and have a butcher's."

"Butcher's, Steeleye?"

"A butcher's hook, Computer, a butcher's hook."

10

"Indeed ... teleport in preparation." The computer raised its logical eyebrow, quite aware that Steeleye liked to feel he was the boss now and again, even if it was a false assumption.

Maybe you don't teleport often, but you must have gone up or down in an elevator, so that you might imagine the sensation of expecting to arrive somewhere and finding when the elevator doors open that you didn't. Not only did you not find a hallway, or a landing, a room or a restaurant, but not an enclosed space at all. When the doors of the elevator opened you found yourself in a field or 300 metres up in the clouds, or on board a battle cruiser, who knows? Steeleye stepped into the teleport chamber and closed his eyes as he normally did. He felt that if he kept his eyes open he might see something he didn't want to see before he re-materialised, while if he only opened them when he had arrived then it would be a bit like Christmas. But this wasn't Christmas. This was Halloween.

"What happened to the fish?" He yelled the question in some vain hope that his launch computer would hear. But his launch was a long way off now, feeling a little deserted. For not only had its Commander disappeared but the strange organic launch before it one moment, was not there the next.

Steeleye stood on a rock, and to one side was grass, long shreds of thick, rough grass that grew across all the other rocks that surrounded him. Not everything was rock though. There was much water too. In fact, most everything was water.

To the other side was an island, standing no more than forty metres at the highest point and about the same across. It had its own waterfall, cascading gently down from a spring rising from the centre.

The island was a jump from where he stood and in between was clear, slightly white water. He moved across the rock outcrop and looked to the horizon. There were other islands, and at a distance of several hundred kilometres a much larger one.

Between them and Steeleye was all water.

The sky was a black-blue, with no visible stars, indeed no visible light source at all. Nevertheless Steeleye could see about him very well. The blue in the high sky changed and merged with a lighter blue and then into a green. One planet was visible, but its shape changed as he watched. It was as though he saw it through a haze of heat, or a ripple of waters. But how could that be? The sphere of a planet could not change shape and there was no sign of a star to give heat waves across the image. And water in space was ridiculous.

The planet sank slowly behind the island, into the water. And all this inside a space launch?

Somehow he had been transported to a world he had not expected ever to see. So . . . could it have been an accident? Could that space launch have been a doorway to this world for chosen people, and not for him? Could it have been a mistake?

No movement touched the water's surface. Steeleye took a molecular sampler from his belt and analysed the liquid as heavy water, or titrium oxide. The atmosphere was thick with humidity too and his sampler told him that it was artificial.

So, what happened on that big island?

Steeleye lifted into the air on his body rockets and drifted slowly and cautiously across the gap, remaining close to the water.

INTER-DEPART-MENTAL MEMORANDUM TO ALL MENTAL-DEPARTS
The–Prince–is–here. Who–will–undertake–the–task?

INTER-DEPART-MENTAL REPLY MEMORANDUM. FROM C3
Not–me – – – after–all–I'm–not–the–jealous–kind– dummy.

DEPART-MENTAL DECISION
AFTER EXTENSIVE DISCUSSIONS WITHIN THE VARIOUS PERSONALITY DEFECTS IT HAS BEEN

DECIDED THAT C3 SHOULD BE APPOINTED TO
UNDERTAKE THE TASK REQUIRED. THIS ORDER
IS SEALED WITH THE APPROVAL OF ALL MEM-
BERS (IN THEIR ABSENCE) SIGNED C1–1000 (Bunch
of lousy absentees) Countersigned by Komast the mighty . . .
er . . . the Mighty.

Ticker ticker.

Thanks–a–lot–buddies.

Everything was coated and wrapped in mildew and moss.
The long-dead pathways were skilfully laid, wall to wall in
a superb green carpet of pure, damp softness.

In some areas there were huge drops of water which fell'
crashing down from the sky. They didn't come from a cloud
formation, but from a hole in the roof!

Everything was encrusted in a thick "crud", laid down
over the years of neglect and damp. The air was humid and
dank about his face, and very soon his entire body was
drenched. He re-erected the force shield about him and sent
a warm blast of air to dry his skin and clothing.

Far more fascinating than all the decay was what lay
under it. For although much of the structural architecture
around him was buried in encrustations, everything stood.
There were no fallen buildings, nothing broken through or
rotted to the ground. It seemed as though everything had
been preserved by the damp air. He stood on a slight
embankment at the side of the water and looked up at the
nearest buildings. They weren't square, or hard edged.
They weren't ordered or even really built at all. They
appeared to have grown from where they stood; to have
intertwined their way from earth to fifty or sixty metres into
the air. Like elaborate mushrooms, their roofs green and
mossed, each dwelling was covered with the bark of trees
and that coated here and there with moss or crud. Stair-
ways had been carved into the materials and wound round
and round through the labyrinth of branches and trunks.
Some of the dwellings were at least 20 metres in diameter
and 10 metres tall, standing very often thirty metres from

13

the ground on a thick and sinuous, twisted tree stump. Fifteen or twenty "houses" were clumped together in sections and then there would be an area of green, with water always flowing everywhere. But no life, or no intelligent life, to be seen.

Steeleye walked up to one of the houses and entered. There were no doors, no locks or shutters, everything was open, and everything coated in damp age.

It was as though the people hid, or had departed suddenly, for nothing had been moved. The small personal belongings were still in place inside the houses; mirrors, tables with plates and combs, bottles and food. Everything spread about, everything coated in condensation and moss ... mildew everywhere.

Steeleye walked out of the house and stared across the open water. Before him lay an empty land, with water stretching as far as he could see. On that land and in that water there was nothing moving, no ripple, no kick of dust, nothing.

It seemed sad, for the place was bursting with fertility and strength, as though the departed life had left behind samples and smells of itself. As though there still survived after what must have been hundreds of years of decay, an atmosphere of life, a breath of potency. But no-one to breathe it, no-one to continue it.

Then the air was disturbed. Steeleye's sensitive skin detected a current around him. It was swirling now, the moisture and dampness had been shifted and was forming new eddies where the mist had hung listlessly before.

Steeleye darted back into the house and looked through the windows into the sky, for up there there had to be something very large to kick up so much movement.

He could see nothing at first, and then a shadow fell over the house, a vast, all embracing shadow that surely came from something bigger than the entire island.

Steeleye moved out into the open more, still taking cover under the mushroomed dwelling. Then he got his first clear view.

A huge winged bird-machine was descending from high

14

in the sky. Its body was metallic, with a tank shape, the nose carrying two huge lights and above them a plate which gave out light from inside. It had massive claws on each side of the body and the wings were so big that they seemed far and away too large, unnecessarily spanning the sky with heavy, lumbering flaps that scattered the air in all directions. The power house of this appalling machine must have been mighty in the least to move those wings, let alone fly the craft with such speed and dexterity, for it soared and skimmed like a light-bodied bird, accustomed to flight.

Its descent wasn't ponderous or clumsy and as it came, Steeleye could see a tall hooded figure standing on the prow surveying the scene below his advance. As it grew closer it swerved about, and the head of the pilot looked down directly towards Steeleye. It would of course be simple for it to find him, for he was, it seemed, the only life on the planet.

There was no escape and somehow, Steeleye did not wish to see the structures around him damaged.

He took off, rising into the sky much higher than the monstrous mechanical bird, which, now that he was closer and level, looked even larger than before. Its wing span must have been 100 metres across and in this confined space it looked even larger than the fish space craft he had encountered in space, though that was three times its size.

The bird turned and thundered at shattering speed towards him, hesitating not one second. It carried guns that shot traces of blaster fire, so that aim was no problem. The trace gave easy direction and Steeleye's force field was battered several times before he moved.

Darting his body at bewildering speed, Steeleye shot underneath the bird and sent a few of his own fire samples up into its belly. His eye glowed sharp red as it fired blast after blast into the very gut of the bird. He severed several of the control lines visible underneath and then shot upward to scream over its head as it attempted to turn and face him.

The pilot had long since ducked down into the body of

15

the ship and was manoeuvring furiously in an attempt to keep at odds with his quarry, but without success.

Until he was lucky. A stray blast caught Steeleye's head through the force field and stunned him momentarily. He fell through fifty metres and hit the soft mossed ground with a sickening thud.

The bird rushed down, its claws open, ready to pinion the prostrate body to the ground.

But Steeleye was still conscious and he turned his body, opened the dreadful steel eye to full aperture and sent a blast that would shiver a planet, into the base of the monstrous bird. The energy needed for that blast drained the strength in his body but it also smashed the monster, intent on his murder.

Its metal belly glowed red and the centre was gone. The wings went limp and the entire structure crumpled as it fell towards the ground. Steeleye rolled his body into the water nearby and swam with what small strength he had to the middle. The machine still had one surprise, for as it fell, just before it should have hit the ground, it vanished.

Steeleye was in no mood for wonderment, only relieved that he would not have to do battle with the pilot. He allowed his exhausted body to float in the heavy water and drifted out across the smooth face of the lake for the water buoyed him up and soothed him. It seemed to take him in its arms so that there was no need for exertion to stay afloat. He felt his burned flesh recover – even as he lay there. And as he lay, he was unaware and uncaring of what was gradually happening to the land. For it was changing, altering its surfaces and features – as though it might be returning to a former shape.

Chapter Three

Then there were voices . . . small, thin voices, children's and female's, that floated across the surface of the water from some distance; gently approaching. Steeleye turned his head and looked. Sure enough there were people wading into the water towards him, waving their arms and shouting. They looked friendly.

Everything else had altered. The moss and crud . . . all the encrustations had gone. The tree houses were new, as though they had cast off the deterioration and dampness. The ground was grass and flower, the moss had gone. The water looked clearer, even where he floated, as though impurities had been filtered out. The sky showed no great falls of water and the air was finer, less dank and heavy.

At least twenty people were wading out towards him and some were swimming now. He remained where he was until the babbling crowd, all female, had swum out the short distance to his side. They chattered excitedly in a language Steeleye could make no sense of and as they laughed and talked they each, five of them, put a soft, leaf-like hammock under Steeleye's body which they tied at top and bottom, to form a cradle on which he was to be transported. They extended the ropes from the corners and each took one and swam back towards the land pulling Steeleye in the makeshift water-bed.

All the time they swam and pulled they chattered, paying little attention to their passenger, as though they already knew him, expecting his arrival.

Once on the shore the floating hammock was pulled up and Steeleye stood on firm ground. His stature was a metre taller than all those who stood about him. All that is, but for one a little way off. There were no males visible, only female adults and children. After a short while the small gathering withdrew and went chattering and laughing into the tree houses.

The female stood, quite still, before Steeleye, as he dried the dampness on his body with the elaborate force shields and convector belts.

"You are Steeleye?" The question was an opener, gently testing his responses.

"Yes, and you ... ?" He faced her now, his usual confidence giving him still more stature. She stood almost 2 metres tall, her hair auburn, thick and plaited against the temples of her head. The design was elaborate and unfamiliar to Steeleye, though not unattractive. She wore a thin piece of silken cloth that fell from the back of her head to shoulder length, draped and held by pins, and her tall perfectly measured body was covered with a similar, fine gossamer, blowing gently about her white limbs. Her face was broad, slavic, though more so, with the eyes so wide apart, Steeleye found them disturbing. Her broad nostrils were negroid and her mouth full and voluptuous. He had noticed other females as he was pulled in, with similar, though much less striking features. She was beautiful, quite beautiful, but that was more a considered opinion than an instinctive attraction at this point.

She stood facing him – the wisp of material blowing. The face was not really welcoming – yet it did not say go away. It was more as though doubt circled within her noble head, knowing not whether to take her fears and cast them into that gently heaving water. For these were two quite strange and alien creatures suddenly confronting one another for the first time.

But she was calm and seemed in no doubt as to his identity.

"I am Lolan, welcome to our planet."

It was as though she delved into his mind as he stood before her – a mighty warrior, his great broad shoulders built to carry any weight, the muscles across his barely covered torso as hard as a breastplate.

He was an immensely impressive figure and his lazy gaze devoured with its constant confidence – the one steel eye

18

forming the only cruel edge, as though this giant in his placid invincibility feared nothing.

"You are invited to remain with us for a time – for there are matters we cannot deal with, matters you may be better equipped to confront."

She spoke without real aggression – not challenging him in any way and not really displaying any resentment at his superior physical stature – but somehow Steeleye felt unwelcome. Her cool eyes were unyielding – the pale but intense blue of the pupils gave little away.

"And I too welcome you, Steeleye." This was a different character – a much older female – her face lined and wise, but open and careless. "My name is Mysemnia – and it was I who brought you here, for Steeleye, we need you. There are problems on Pensil that cannot easily be solved even by the Prince of Fire himself."

Like a smoothly sophisticated guest Steeleye gently spread his broad hands, placed one on each of their delicate shoulders and sat with them on the water's edge.

The clothing that Lolan wore showed her body completely through its transparent fineness and as he sat, Steeleye admired the soft fall of her breasts and the turn of the pink nipples upon them.

He saw that her race, quite unfamiliar to him, was similar in physical appearance to that of Woman. There were children sitting in the tree houses and on the branches of the trees, looking down upon this strange creature, brought to their shores. They swung their legs lazily and occasionally looked out at the water, scampered back into the houses, or swung like accomplished gibbons about the branches.

"Pensil is in the galaxy of Waterspace. You will have questions to ask about the nature of our world."

"Are you all of one gender on Pensil?"

"Yes . . . there is no other gender to our species. We are self-reproducing. Indeed each species on this planet and all those in Waterspace can reproduce all the other species. I can give birth either to a child, or a flower or an animal. I am equipped to do all these things. So too, I can fertilise another species with seeds or pollen that are made in me."

19

"That is unique."

Mysemnia sat, silently observing Steeleye as Lolan spoke with him. Her dress was quite different, the old, drooped shoulders sloped under with a huge beautifully coloured cloak that seemed to float about her though the material was thick and heavy. There were no two parts of similar colour – some of the variations were new even to Steeleye who had seen the Rainbows of Casalshimas, where colour was infinite.

Her face was old – the kind of age that has ceased to count time – and her hair fell in wispy shapeless locks, surrounding strange features, large and melancholy – disfigured with wisdom.

"We are unique people." Lolan's look was always querying as though she expected him to refuse them help at any time.

"Lolan is unsure of you, Steeleye. You must be patient with her – for she will reward you for your indulgence. We have suffered thus far and will suffer yet. I shall leave you now to walk together. I grow tired – the years take their toll – as you will learn Steeleye. Enjoy yourself now – there are many wonders to see here." And Mysemnia drifted away from them.

Lolan rose gracefully from the ground and led Steeleye by the hand across a shallow stretch of water and up on to a narrow bank.

In the centre of the island stood a huge, knotted tree, curving and twisted.

"This is called an Ottertree. Watch, for soon it will bear offspring."

The branches were covered in lumps and gnarled curves and on one under side a large cyst hung down, covered in the bark, but thicker than the rest. As they stood watching the bulge cracked down the centre and into a "Y" shape at each end. It measured 30 centimetres and curved under the tree about 15 centimetres. As the fabric of the bark cracked and snapped it seemed to obey natural laws.

It opened. Each end peeled back like soft claws, five fingers of fur on the inside, bark on the outside. The inside

20

was covered in feathery hairs, thousands of them, making a soft cocoon – thick like the coat of a new born chick. Each finger was clutching the claws of an animal that had been its precious burden. The fingers of the animal were freed and it fell the metre to the ground, its body twisting as it went, the feet, drawn in perfect opposition to the edges of the womb and, as the hands let go, it landed softly.

It was like an Otter, with beautiful brown fur, specked with stripes of grey and silver. The head unfolded from the chest as it fell and the body was long and snake-like.

As it landed the feet were already scampering and it spurted away into the longer grass.

"That was a Treeotter . . . born of the Ottertree, naturally."

"Naturally . . ." Steeleye walked up to the tree and laid a careful hand upon the open womb. As he touched it, though his fingers were gentle, it contracted and drew in the extended claws of the bark stroking his fingers as it closed. He stood, one hand leaning against the tree, looking out over the water. Watching an animal born of a tree now was so logical that it seemed extraordinary that he had not witnessed it before.

He stepped away from the tree and as he did so, the toe of one foot stepped upon a thick, much more springy piece of grass. He stooped down and laid his hand in the thick, bushy, very soft patch about a metre square and directly below the otter's birthplace. Nature's cushion to comfort the fall of its child.

"Everything in Waterspace is alive, Steeleye – everything is co-ordination – for we are ruled by our galaxy – by the water itself."

"This water?" Steeleye swept a hand across the surrounding waters of the island.

"Yes, but more than that – you see – our galaxy – our space – is not space at all – it is not a vacuum like yours – but water."

"Water? In space – but that's – well – extraordinary."

"Well – it may be – but it keeps us alive and here – we could not live without it."

21

Steeleye looked up at the sky – like a child trying to understand the stars.

"Our planets are protected by artificial atmospheric shields – powered by the movement of Waterspace – as is everything else. Our crops, our light, our heat, everything. Come – carry me to the island you arrived upon and I will take you back to the bio-launch where you can see the beauty of our world for yourself."

Whether through pride at her surroundings or a lessening of uncertainty, Lolan seemed to be warming to Steeleye and as his great arms lifted her and carried her slight body into the air he could feel the smooth, tender warmth of her skin against him. Her arm about his shoulder though, still held him slightly aloof.

The air was good – free and clear – as they flew swiftly over the islands and waters of Pensil. It was a world at least 90% water though in some patches two islands would be quite close and the great sprouting tree leaves had made a bridge across, joining hands high above the water. Steeleye could see small, running creatures and animals scampering to and fro amongst a community set high above the two islands.

There were always people swimming and paddling in the water and in some parts, as they skimmed over – large groups were ceremoniously dunking themselves – in a mass baptism. Off other islands there would be swimmers, sometimes hundreds of metres from a land mass – and boats, small canoes, lazy row boats, sailing boats and paddle boats surrounding and moored from the islands. Nobody was very troubled by life – no-one concerned to discover problems; like children of isolation – who have been spoken to only of happiness.

Steeleye set Lolan down upon the rocky island where he had first met Pensil. Nothing was changed – even the ripples of the falling spring looked unchanged.

"Now from here we teleport into the launch. Are you ready?"

She stood before him, the fine covering about her slender body like whispers of delight – floating in the caressing air.

22

"Yes – some more of your magic." She took his hand in hers, the fingers pressing the warm, dry flesh of his muscled palms – tenderly communicating. And Steeleye felt the familiar jolt within his body, closing his eyes, as his body dematerialised and reformed.

Opening them *was* a surprise – like they say, an unexpected pleasure – for this time he got a look inside the launch he had previously hoped to investigate.

Now the average – or indeed even sub-standard flight specifications demand – under normal circumstances a few artfully displayed control panels – designed unobtrusively – to give the space traveller a feeling of home – to obscure images of emptiness within the phenomenon of space. But simultaneous to this primary need there had to be visible means of driving a space launch – I mean – it's OK to feel at home – but you aren't going to leave it without at least a speedo gauge or two. OK – so this was not normal circumstances – but inside this launch there were no controls – no banked equipment – no electro-systems – just beautiful deep-cushioned seats – small, smooth topped tables and an entertainment console with selections from features, libraries, love scenes – you choose.

"Ah ha – " Steeleye gasped. "I see a control – a renegade switch – come let me clutch thee." But it was only a drink dispenser – and Steeleye had one – a drink that is.

"Well – nice little place you got here." The walls were covered in fine, soft hairs – like the inside of the Ottertree's womb, and across the front was a broad screen that looked out upon the stars.

Lolan smiled at his flippancy – the first real smile he had seen. Her broad eyes creased and deep dimples formed in her cheeks – it was a face, almost, that cleared its tensions – as though much had been hidden from those upon which it gazed – and just this once there was calm. She troubled Steeleye.

"Come, Steeleye – for so big a man you clown with grace. Sit – for we are going on a short trip to see Waterspace – from the outside."

"So, this launch is still in the space I left it?"

23

"Yes."

"Why did you put it here?"

"I didn't – Mysemnia laid the trap for you – she chose Ghost Space because she knew it would all the more intrigue you."

"I see – and now we must travel back to Waterspace –"

"Yes – but to the outside instead."

There was no sound or movement. No thrust of power, no time jolts – just warm comfort.

"Please tell me how we go." Steeleye continued to search for some means of control.

"We are in the body of a living organism – this launch thinks for herself – she moves by her own power – controls her own destination and computes her own journey – she takes her orders from my thoughts – and that is all she needs." She lazed upon the cushioned rests.

"I see." Steeleye gave up the search and did likewise.

"She has wings you see – which vibrate."

"Yes – I saw them – they were very beautiful – "

"Ah – everything in Waterspace is beautiful."

"You too." Steeleye stared open faced at her. She did not flinch but looked back at him, the pale, certain eyes gleaming and flashing, the lids heavy and deep.

INTER-DEPART-MENTAL MEMORANDUM. FROM ALL DEPARTMENTS EXCEPT C3 TO C3

You–cocked–that–up–proper–didn't–you–you–no–good –personality–defect–you. Nowaddarwedo?

INTER-DEPART-MENTAL MEMORANDUM FROM C3 TO ALL DEPART-MENTALS

Bird-bashing?

DEPART-MENTAL DECISION. MEMORANDUM TO ALL DE-PARTS.

AFTER EXTENSIVE DISCUSSION WITH ALL

DEPARTING AND MENTAL PARANOIDS IT HAS BEEN DECIDED THAT THE MECHA-TANKS SHALL BE SENT OUT TO DO SOME DAMAGE ... TE HE. SIGNED BY ALL MEMBERS (Always present for a communal thrashing.)

"We shall soon be there – then you will see our unique Waterspace. Come – the view is better from the Gods." She raised a delicate hand above her head and swept it gaily through the air, taking Steeleye's hand with the other.

He felt a cool shield slip about his body, and above their heads – slightly in front, the roof of the launch slid back and opened displaying the black cloth – dotted with silver holes. They floated out and as they went Lolan said, "Close your eyes, Steeleye, close them tight ... I will guide your way ... come."

Steeleye felt he was being led by a benevolent fairy god-mother who took her charge to some hidden magic world.

"You can open your eyes now." They were still now, on top of the launch ... Steeleye could feel the soft furry hull under him as he opened his eyes and looked.

The Heavens of Waterspace were visible ... not as a whole, but as a top surface of water ... like a lake. The lake was in space, standing in empty deep space, unaided and rippling like it was the most natural thing you ever imagined. There were no waves as such, no steady movement, only a gentle drift as though someone were blowing a simple breeze across the surface continuously.

The water was black, tinged with green ... not dirty, indeed the top surface shone like a newly polished ice rink, but with a darkened hue that said depth ... wow, depth wasn't in it, this piece of water was 16 parsecs deep ... that's 50 light years expanse of water, nothing but water. And there was no pressure, no gravity, so that nothing could be crushed within it. Just as nothing in deep space will crush you. Water in its free state, without the pressures of matter exerted upon it is as free and light as a vacuum.

Steeleye blew out a puff of his amazement and Lolan caught it.

"That is our galaxy.... We think it's a very special galaxy, it gives you a good feeling to look at it ... doesn't it?"

"It makes me ... well, like space never did, like a million light years never worried me, this makes me feel small, insignificant."

"Well, that's fine ... it is not common to see so much water gathered in one place."

"It must be unique."

"Well, not if you look sideways ... this galaxy exists in 84 points to either side in the Dimen structures. It also exists in less adequate forms over 3000 dimens ... the farthest we have seen is point 3011 where it falls off to an unstable formation of part Deutronic Oxide and part H_2O, one proton. Nothing can live in that because it gives no life."

"Life? You mean this water feeds you as well?"

"Yes, it gives us everything we have. A constant cross-fertilisation. Everything."

"How, how can water give food?"

"By living. Waterspace is alive."

"You mean it contains spores and creatures that are alive?"

"No, I mean that the water is alive, the atoms have formed into a structure that can support a sensitive intelligence en masse."

"So when you said everything was alive you meant it literally?"

"Yes, Waterspace contains every conceivable food form, it is like a massive fertile earth, with a molecular structure encompassing every chemical needed to support life in its womb, supporting its children with a placenta of nutrition. We want for nothing."

Steeleye remained still, and silent.

He had sat on the beaches of warm climates where they say the air and the sea combine to make music and he had swum in sea where the waters cleanse the conscience. Many worlds that were surrounded by water, drowned in water, yet nowhere had he even contemplated so much water – so much, so calm, so forbidding. As he had said a million light years of space was just emptiness – but this was more mystical and powerful than anything he had ever encountered.

There were sounds here too – singing across the water. A cool mixture of melodious improvisations. The sound was mesmeric.

"You hear our voices – our music?"

"Yes, what is it?"

"It is The Alter's Call – when our people first came to Waterspace they were confronted as you are, by this sight and sound. And their leader, our first leader was named Alter, she was a strange creature – powerful and unbending in her rule of her people – but one of great mystical belief – and superstition. She would come here in stressful times and call the waters to help her."

Lolan paused – "They say that sound is her voice and that it gives us warning."

"Does it only sound when there's danger?" Steeleye listened.

"Do you believe such things, Steeleye – you – the Prince of Time?"

"Of course – haven't you noticed how the mystical is always constant – superstition always means something – even if it isn't exactly what you imagine."

"Then what should I beware?"

"I don't know Lolan – yourself perhaps?" Steeleye did not look at her – his eyes absorbed by the magic of Waterspace. They were silent for a time. Then they turned and looked upon one another, and in her face Steeleye saw and accepted pain and doubt – much fear lurked there, behind those heavy lidded eyes but at last she began to smile and soften to this great giant.

"I have a signal, Steeleye, something is wrong on Pensil. ... We must return, come."

They returned to the launch and Lolan spoke with lightning instructions to set the craft back to the surface. Within seconds they were standing again on the rocks.

"Oh WaterGods, what have they done?" She screamed at the air as Steeleye looked up and saw dozens of the huge clawed, mechanical birds moving over their heads away from the islands.

"Carry me ... carry me to the islands quickly.... They have killed again. We must help, quickly, before it is too late."

Steeleye swept her up and raced the short distance across the water as the birds escaped into the atmosphere. As they approached he could see that bodies lay strewn about the ground and floated in the water. Lolan leapt from his arms and rushed to the nearest.

"Help me, help me.... Get them together. Put them all in the water quickly, please."

She was frantic with anger and pain, her body shaking. She cried and trembled as she picked the heavy bodies from where they lay and tossed them into the water, all the time shouting at Steeleye to do the same.

He was able, because of his size and strength to carry several of the prostrate dead at one time, using his force projectors as well as his powerful arms to take them up and lay them gently into the water. And after what seemed a long and stressful battle, they had succeeded in immersing all the bodies of the people into the now rippling and bubbling lake. Steeleye stood at the side breathing heavily from his exertion. Anguished and doubtful, they watched as the last of the bodies sunk slowly beneath the surface.

Lolan sat by the lake side, dejected, utterly forlorn.

Steeleye stepped towards her, but as he was about to put a reassuring arm about her delicate, muscled shoulder, she stood and with a dreadful note of anger and vengeance cursed the air above them.

"Komast ... I challenge you.... Come again now you coward.... Come again to my land and kill the way you kill.... Take our lives.... Now that we have a champion to fight you Komast.... Come again.... You will die and you will die forever.... For you are the only decay in Waterspace.... We shall all live again ... but when you are crushed Komast you will be gone for all time."

Her voice lifted, reverberating the air like ten voices and by way of reply came a shattering crash of thunder from the sky which shook the ground. Lolan stood still and unaffected. They remained silent for several minutes, Steeleye staring sadly out over the now darkening lakes, Lolan sat, her knees pulled up, head bent, breathing softly.

And night came on Pensil.

Chapter Four

In the night, within the soft security of the tree house Lolan told Steeleye of the plight of her people. Laid gently upon his great shoulder, her arms tucked within his strength and under soft feathered blankets, she was as she had been in the foetal arms of her birth place, speaking only in a whisper to the champion brought to save them.

"We had lived here . . . all of us . . . and more . . ." Her voice was so quiet Steeleye drew closer to her soft mouth.

"During hundreds of years . . . those years . . . without event."

Long pauses broke her words and Steeleye felt the lethargy of exhaustion drift through his body, her gentle warmth spreading.

"We had more than we needed and without the pains and disquiet of discovery and experience we lived a wise life. There was never any need . . . for us to learn . . . we were given learning . . . we had no requirements . . . no demands . . . we knew not how to ask . . . for everything came before we spoke."

She paused and a great heavy breath sucked in her lungs and gushed out.

"It was the goodness of gifts, bestowed without malice or envy. Bestowed by an intelligent and caring love that had no selfish designs upon us . . . the love of Waterspace, until Komast came to disturb our calm. Komast the Colossus' master . . . Komast killer . . . Komast the mortal."

Silence sent Steeleye's mind drifting back to the emptiness of this world when he first arrived and the dreadful mechanical birds that had returned after the first abortive attempt on his life.

Now they had taken less defended lives and a sting of anger shot through Steeleye's body.

Lolan felt his tenseness, and knew his thoughts.

"Your anger is ours, Steeleye, do not spend it except on Komast, for he is ready to be fought . . . now. He is ready for you . . . and you will need the full extent of your powers for he is wily and old . . . he has crushed many enemies and beaten back those who would call themselves strong . . . and he has Colossus to help him."

"What is Colossus?"

"Colossus is our own computer, an organic computer, built to serve us. It has a vast and complex brain but its power centres and memory divertors were too strong for its collective capacity. It's almost funny I suppose, but it has a split personality."

Steeleye laughed slightly, his chest moving with the gentle humour.

"You have everything here . . . even a living computer . . . as if that were not enough, it has to be schizoid too."

"Yes, that is right . . . a schizophrenic computer . . . it has 1000 personalities, Steeleye, and they are all crazy."

She laughed out loud for the first time, and turned to Steeleye.

"Show me how you kiss on your world . . . kiss me now."

Steeleye touched her full soft mouth with his.

"So strong, but you give softness too."

She kissed him again and slid her small strong hands down his body.

"This is new for me, Steeleye. I have never known such things . . . you must be careful, be careful."

Steeleye felt himself lifted, as though by her volition. He was light, eager but gentle, passionate and yet able to think only of her wishes and give the greater part of their divided pleasure to the small tender body beneath him. Tender she might have been but her muscle and the power of her natural strength was great. She exerted her smooth hips about him, pulling and thrusting upon him, giving without ever having given in such a way before. Steeleye found he had soon lost all control, drowning in this creature of Waterspace.

Then they lay still, returned to their entwined position,

31

silent. Steeleye drifted into a deep and gentle sleep. He knew exactly where he was and how he slept. He could see himself . . . like a traveller on the astral plain . . . looking down upon his body from above. He knew that he slept . . . and yet he did not . . . for now Lolan was taking his hand and leading him back over the tortured years of Waterspace to see the beginning of Komast.

They stood together upon a beach . . . a small island, like their own. They stood arm in arm, her hands twisting fingers into his, her body leaning slightly against him and one foot gently perched upon the other . . . and in this style they watched the past deliver its story.

The sky was bleak and dangerous . . . as though the weather were angry. The greyness loomed down upon the island and the waters boiled and gurgled around it.

The trees were only small and the tree houses, when Steeleye first saw them, huge and dominant, were now smaller and carrying only five or six dwellings. Everything looked younger, fresher, less lived in . . . as though life had only just stepped into these shoes and tucked its arms into this coat.

"We are three hundred years in our past, Steeleye."

"And how old were you then?" Steeleye asked, turning his head to hers and nuzzling her soft auburned hair.

"I was only a child . . . soon grown from the waters. . . ."

And sure enough round from the back of the tree houses stepped a small, slender form . . . a child of no more than ten years and in the likeness of Lolan . . . indeed, of course, it was Lolan herself.

The girl Lolan did not see them, for they were not there. She stepped lightly across the sanded earth, touching her toes to the ground first, treading like a practised ballet dancer, her hands folded behind – the shoulders pulled back, shoulder blades almost touching. She looked into the waters, and then at the skies. She stood still a moment and then stepped around, facing the opposite way . . . as though awaiting a visitor who had not reported her direction of approach. But nothing came.

She stood with her legs apart, the small thin feet slanted

on their sides, her body swaying from the trunk. Thus she remained during a long time.

"That's me, Steeleye ... do you realise it's really me ..." Lolan spoke with amazement, and delight.

"And this is your childhood home." Steeleye watched the sky nervously.

"There is nothing you can do here to change what happens ... this is time recounted ... we are not actually here ... we are but spectators of a film."

And as they watched the skies grew still darker ... filled with doom and forboding. Lolan instinctively grasped Steeleye's arm tighter and drew her warm face against his shoulder. Steeleye, for his part tightened his muscles and narrowed his eyes, waiting for what was to come. But it was not so ... not so at all.

Upon the island were hundreds of young ... mostly scattered about the island and in the water on the other side, just visible from where Lolan and Steeleye watched the child Lolan.

"Were they your people?" Steeleye asked.

"Yes ... they were my people then ... but watch and see where my anger derives."

And as he watched a cloud filled the sky ... a dull, murky cloud, more brown than black, more stirring than undulating, more gorged than pregnant.

It drove like a relentless machine towards the island ... moving quite steadily, forward and down. It reached a point only a few moments from the island and Steeleye could see that it was not energy or a real cloud, but a kind of floating space container. It measured no more than 10 metres across and on its back it was carrying something. Something that looked like strands of rope all lashed together. It stopped above the island and hesitated ... looking down upon the frightened children.

And from its interior came a small machine, a biped ... its body short and squat, its head small. It descended to a distance about one metre from the ground and then shifted gear and sped towards the children. In its metal hand it grasped three children and whipped them off the ground,

33

like they were leaves fresh fallen from an autumn tree. The metal appendage dug into the young flesh and gashed them, drawing great quantities of blood which dripped into the waters about the island.

The machine, somehow, almost by magic, had tied pieces of rope about their necks and was rapidly lassooing them to trees nearby. This done, it still held the children up in its massive arms. Then, with one ceremonious move the robot dropped them all ... so that their bodies swung on the branches and they were strangled.

The child Lolan let out a hideous tortured scream ... and the monstrous killer robot turned its metallic head toward the sound. There was something so bitterly cold and brutal about the killings. It is hard to imagine murder in any event ... when performed by the living ... but a machine that deals out death is more frightful still for it walks the earth casting life aside like a foot smothers the dust.

There were now ten small females strung up in the air, hanging from trees ... unable to get back to their precious water to sustain them ... gone for ever, with no hope of re-life.

Lolan was not simply horrified ... she was furiously angry and her body writhed with the tremors of revenge.

She stepped back from the advancing robot, now intent on stringing her body beside her islander friends and loves.

She moved to a nearby tree stump and spoke to the tree.

"Give me a branch that I may protect myself ... and fight this killer who comes to destroy our happiness."

At once the tree laid a branch upon her upturned hand and she plucked it from the bark. It was heavy wood, a kind of mahogany.

She wielded it ferociously as the robot advanced. The mechanical creature could not measure more than two metres and was not therefore so great a battle challenge to her. And she had the aid of her tree.

As the robot approached the tree lifted a root and the great robot took a tremendous tumble, crashing to the ground unceremoniously.

Lolan raised the hefty club and brought it down with

34

massive force upon the head and neck of the robot. It squawked and grabbed her legs. But, retaining her cool, she raised the club once more ... delivering a blow this time which would have felled a bison. The robot collapsed and Lolan set about opening the plate that controlled the motor power source.

She put a hand into the opening and Steeleye winced for fear she would be bolted to the ground by a shock from the power source ... but she wrenched her fist out, pulling half the robot's circuits with it. She set about beating the death out of the thing until it was a mashed pile of rubbish lying upon the ground.

"Some girl."

"Yes ... lot of muscle."

The girl Lolan then began the morbid task of lowering the bodies from their gibbets. Each time she brought one down, she slid the limp body into the water and returned for the next.

"Is that where you bury them?" Steeleye asked.

"In a manner ... yes ... you will see when we return."

The skies were still dull and grey and behind Lolan now ... appeared a male creature ... looking like a man, though sturdier of build ... with thick short legs and a balding head. The body had no bottom or waist ... the trunk straight and fat. The legs so short that they buckled and bowed like a dwarf.

He was dwarfed by Lolan who stood a full metre taller, but this did not advantage her, for his strength was great. He approached Lolan and, frowning heavily, began to speak in an evil voice, the sound waves blasting across the waters as though he wished to be heard throughout the planet.

There would be no disobedience or undermining orders ... Pensil and all the planets of Waterspace were now his.

Lolan was aghast.... "You mean you did that ... deliberately ... you sent your robot and killed those children. ... You slaughtered them just as a demonstration."

"That is correct." He remained quite unmoved.

It was as though a poison had entered the kingdom of

Waterspace ... as though a festering filth had dripped through and suddenly grown to become Lord and master. And Lolan could not imagine what she was to do.

"I see you have smashed my robot."

Lolan, the young Lolan looked down upon the twisted pieces of metal that lay strewn about the ground.

"Yes ... but I smashed the wrong head."

"Come, come now child ... do not grow bitter ... what are a few deaths. There will be many more ... if you do not co-operate ... for I have other machines to kill ... young and old ... and if they fail under your powerful hand then I shall kill without their help."

He advanced upon her. "And when I kill, I kill with my bare hands."

Lolan swung the club with everything she'd got left in her anger and terror and the end connected with a sickening crunch with the creature's head. It cracked open and a ghastly green, yellow pus spewed out in rivers. ...

It kept on coming. ... And the body remained standing, leaning forward, allowing the muck to pour out, gallon after gallon of it, until it was about her feet. Screaming and shivering with this unbearable foulness, Lolan ran from the scene ... and as she ran the voice of the creature ran after her.

"You can run Lolan ... you can run forever, and you will never escape ... for I am Komast the killer ... Komast, the poisoned one. And I am here to take your planet and your galaxy for my own ... I do not care how long it needs ... I shall be ready ... and you Lolan shall be the vessel for my conception and birth into this new life ... never forget ... for your body will nurture my new growth ... one day Lolan ... one day."

'My Holy Father.' Steeleye muttered. 'I'd give a few credits to get my hands on him."

"Oh, there will be plenty of opportunity for that, Steeleye, plenty ... for he is still with us ... in all his many shapes. ... Come ... I will show you another. ..."

This time they stood together amongst the ruined, moss

covered remains of the island where Steeleye had first found himself. There was no sign of life, and everything looked long gone ... years of buried civilisation. They were back in the time disbursement again.

The trees were fallen and splintered and the waters dried out. Faint in the distance came the sound of an echoed laughter ... an eerie sound that seemed to ripple through the atmosphere as it grew closer. From one of the empty and battered, crud-filled doorways came a small slender figure. A young Lolan, though not so young as before. She was quite petrified ... shaking with anxiety. Treading stealthily through the musky deadness of her once lively world, she stopped each time the laughter sounded about her.

Steeleye and Lolan stood together, he clutching her tenderly to his powerful body. They watched the suffering of Lolan's past as she faced the torture and persecution of Komast once more. This time he appeared in another manifestation ... as a huge bird, that flapped noisily down from the sky and landed some fifty metres from where Lolan hid.

The bird was at least twenty times her size and its body, black and greased, shone with muscle and thick, grimy feathers. It flapped slightly, adjusting its wings, clucking about the ground. The blinking, glazed, pupil-less eyes, popped open and shut, and the lids fell back into place with a hideous coldness.

The coldness of brainless stupidity. ... Komast made a perfect bird ... utterly stupid, small headed, heavy bodied.

Lolan took a large rock in her plucky hand and hurled it to the other side of the island. The ridiculous bird turned its head and scampered off toward the sound. Lolan moved stealthily through the broken buildings, searching for she knew not what.

For this change in her land was inescapable ... she could not escape until she was returned to her own time.

There was a scraping sound. Lolan, still young and tender, whirled about and picked up another piece of the water's encrustation, in her soft unaccustomed hand.

The bird stood, no more than two metres away from her, blowing up a gust of wind as it flapped its thick hideous wings. It placed one webbed, clawing foot forward and raised the other. It came down with a crash . . . disdainful and careless of Lolan's presence nearby. One claw caught her thin clothing and ripped it completely. But not quite off her body. She was trapped by the anchored claw, that grasped thoughtlessly at the material, still wound, but now much more tightly, about her neck. She lifted the stone in her hand and brought it down with as much strength as she could muster, upon the foot . . . that nasty black claw. The bird squawked and blood, or some thick red liquid oozed from a great gash across the claws. It lifted, but the material was still attached and Lolan was carried into the air with the moving claw. She was being raised higher and higher, towards the beak.

And poor terrified Lolan had no escape from a dreadful fate.

She wriggled and tossed herself in the inadvertent grip, pulling viciously so that her own body was cut and gashed by the material, straining to tear enough to release her. And as she was drawn ever nearer to the great beak, it broke at last and she was cast without thought to the hard ground, where she lay unconscious.

And the night came on. And still she remained. The bird had gone. But soon, as the light began to return a tall, white dressed creature came towards the prone body. The woman moved closer and bent, kneeling beside the mutilated body. And she dipped her hand to her side, leaning over far, dipping her whole arm, as though the ground where she knelt was not hard crust at all, but liquid. As the hand pulled out from the ground it came with cupped water, white, thick water, which she transferred on to Lolan's head, wetting her forehead gently and with such care and love. And she repeated the performance . . . somehow gathering this water from her time, to touch and quench Lolan's wounds. And as she did so, she spoke quietly to herself.

"My poor child . . . so you suffer by his hand once more

... and you will suffer again ... oh Lord of Waterspace, why can you not help us ... why can you not send a bolt of power to destroy this creature that seeks to destroy us ... and soon will succeed ..." And she cried silently as she bathed Lolan's broken body.

And again she spoke.

"Colossus, you too are gone from us ... you too have betrayed us ... is there no help you will give ... to save your faithful people?"

And there was no answer, either from Waterspace or from Colossus.

And still she went on bathing the child Lolan.

"Who is she?" Steeleye asked as they observed the creature.

"That is my mother ... our Queen.... See how she weeps."

And the picture faded.

Steeleye sat up sharply in the slender bed, his huge leg dangling over the edge.

"How come it's morning....?"

Lolan was not in the room, but as he spoke she returned and stood beside him, smiling slightly.

"Come outside and see my people ... they are returning ... one by one."

Steeleye was led out of the tree house and down the steps. As he descended he could already see some movement in the water around the island.

"Who are they?"

"The dead, Steeleye, the dead. ..." She pulled his hand and tugged him down to the sanded edge. From the water came young slender girls, no more than ten years of age, all quite naked, walking out of the water smiling at Steeleye and Lolan.

"Welcome back ..." She held out her hands and each that came from the water touched her and kissed her cheek.

Soon there were twenty come out, and still more broke the surface, and rose up, as though they had simply walked from the other island. Eventually all had returned. All young girls, all going to their homes in the tree houses and taking up their lives as though they had never ended.

"They are young again, very young," Steeleye asked.

"Yes ... whenever Komast sends his Mecha-Tanks to kill us our people die and rise again as children ... it is very easy for them ... though it is not pleasant to lose your life."

"So why does he bother?"

"Because he is angry that he can do no great harm and because he knows also that he does do harm. He saps our energies, he depletes us and he makes our adults into children. Most of all he hopes to kill me."

"Why?"

"Because I lead them all here ... as do others on each of the islands, and if he kills us then there will be no-one to say 'no' to him."

"What is it that he wants so badly?"

They sat on the sand and the new children brought food and fruit, and poured a soft drink that sent Steeleye's head spinning gently.

Lolan sighed heavily and turned her head from Steeleye, looking out over the water, feeling the small breeze on her face.

"Komast is a poison ... a force ... perhaps you might say he is a river, trying hard to flow into our ocean, and we will not let him ... we cannot let him ... and because of that he will stagnate, silt up, strangle himself with his own decay, and eventually die.

"He has travelled for millions of years through the Universe – long lost to his birth place. They say he grew from an element that became misplaced within his Universe – a substance that began to destroy and did not contribute. So, like so many that cannot survive, he was ousted by the strength of his opponents."

She sat silently for a moment – her eyes sad for her enemy.

"He seems to have drifted through eternity before coming here – and gathered all the poison on the way – never finding good – like a rolling ball of dirt – a river gathering silt."

"I don't understand ... what do you mean, he is a river ... a force ... you mean he's water like your own galaxy?"

40

"In a way, yes ... except that he's not actually water ... his elements are Amonic ... a complex mixture of substance which I do not believe could happily co-exist on Zrost ... it is known as Sascorbia and its elemental contacts resemble Ammonia with various arsenical forms which we had previously never come across. It is ... at any rate ... toxic and cannot be tolerated in Waterspace. Indeed should he be permitted to flow into our galaxy we would survive perhaps ... for three days."

"But Waterspace is vast ... how could it be so poisoned by just a river?"

"A river of Sascorbia can poison a universe ... its properties are more active than a virulent disease ... Komast *is* a virulent disease. You cannot go near him, nor touch him. A mere splash from his mouth will kill you instantly, should he wish it."

"He takes different forms then?"

"Yes ... he takes many forms ... but there is no need for our benefit for he merely uses poor dear old Colossus and the Mecha-Tanks. We built them many years ago when we needed to defend ourselves occasionally from outside attack. Now they are turned against us."

"And against me."

"You? When?" She turned and looked up at Steeleye.

"When you found me in the water, I was there because I had fought with one, none of this was here."

"Ah, a time disturbance ... that is another of Colossus' little games ... our computer was well equipped with little games. I am sorry that you should be subjected to such a poor welcome."

"You have more than made up for that." He smiled at her.

They sat in silence for a moment and then Steeleye turned to Lolan.

"But tell me of these time disturbances."

"Oh – it is merely a trick. Colossus carries records of time. She can tap the past and from it she can select a small detail – like a portion of a painting – and disturb it from its own time and position the molecular structures in the

41

presten. So – she removes a grass bank or a portion of water and replaces it with something from the past – sculpted by her to fit exactly like a jig-saw puzzle."

"Clever – and simple. I wonder what could be made of it? . . . Where is my launch?"

"I will take you to it . . . will it help us?"

"Yes . . . I have a computer too . . . a mechanical, very dead one . . . though I would never say that to its face."

"So . . . like all those who live, you imagine life in the dead. And you are right . . . for your computer lives as much as you do . . . in a manner . . . for all molecules move, all atoms disturb . . . everything that moves, lives."

"Your philosophy is fascinating." They walked side by side to the other end of the island.

"It is not merely a philosophy, Steeleye . . . it is a fact . . . as much as the knowledge that death is the inescapable beginning of life. Your people . . . the race of man . . . I have read, and visioned much about them . . . they believed in the sanctity of death . . . they believed that death was special. Am I not right?"

"Yes, I suppose that is correct."

"Well, they cared much for the dead . . . burial, grave-yards, heaven and hell, God, tombs, much fuss."

"Yes . . . and what do you make of it?" Steeleye walked with his great hands clasped behind his back in the manner of an attentive professor.

"Well, I think that Man understood exactly what death was all about . . . but because he feared it . . . because his knowledge was surrounded in suspicion and cross pur-pose . . . so also he surrounded his understanding and his appreciation of death with apparatus . . . with trappings . . . as if to say well . . . yes . . . I do know what it's all about. But . . . let's take out some insurance in case. . . ."

"So what should he have done?"

"Simple . . . allowed the dead to come back to life again."

She spoke with such steady naivety that Steeleye found himself wondering why on Earth it had never happened this way.

In reply he smiled at her upturned face.

42

"So simple . . ."

"As simple as a heart beat. . . ."

"When all this is over and the problems solved, perhaps you will come back with me to Earth in the 22nd century and then we will show them how it is done. . . ."

"And what will that achieve?"

"Well, you will become the second . . . or would it be the third, Messiah . . ."

They laughed . . . deriding a dead race.

They stepped inside the massive launch . . . or so it appeared, now settled on the land.

"Computer?"

"Yes, Steeleye . . ."

"You mean you don't have a name for your computer? . . . No, that will not do . . . here in Waterspace, everything has a name . . . part of the identity you understand. . . . Now what would the computer like to be called? . . . Tell me, Computer, what is your favourite name?"

"I think that it would aid the conversation, Steeleye, if you were to introduce your guest to me." The computer retained a formal tone.

"Computer . . . about to be renamed. . . . Please welcome the island leader of Pensil in the galaxy of Waterspace, Lolan."

"Welcome . . . Lolan . . . were it not already taken I would have chosen your name for myself."

"Ah, you have a fancy computer Steeleye, charming . . . now, come, what is your favourite name . . . aside from Lolan?"

"Well . . . I feel that I am male . . . and I am something of a sentimental old thing . . . I remember the name of the very first character that Steeleye came into contact with outside the planet of the Eumigs . . . his name was Tarash. . . ."

"No good . . . much too harsh . . . think again," said Lolan.

"I see that my will is not to be my own. . . ." The computer almost chortled.

43

"No question, Computer ... you must choose a name that is appropriate to its birth place."

"Very well ... wait and I will examine my dictionary of Designations ... recorded from the very best source."

"Oh? Where?"

"Afractua. Among the items I made use of during your early visit there was the enormous video library of names. Please be patient ... it will take me three seconds to peruse."

And three seconds it was.

"Taking into account the restrictions placed upon my choice by those present and the environment in which I find myself ... I have narrowed the availables down to three ... Grifalbo ... Dorian ... and Benerinda ..."

Steeleye and Lolan laughed so much that the computer prepared to apply life support systems.

"Ridiculous ... ridiculous ... I have never heard such names ... I dread to think what the rejections were like. ... Come now, I shall name you myself ... you shall be called ... English."

"English? ... What in the name of cybernetics is English?"

"You are ... English ... and that is your name ... let that be an end to it."

"I protest."

"The days of Computer Liberation have not yet reached your section ... English ..." Steeleye laughed at his computer's discomfort.

"Hmph. ... I hope you're not expecting to acquire too much information from my banks for the next few years."

"Oh, dear ... I was rather hoping ..."

"Then you can hope ... this computer is in a sulk."

"Uh ..." Steeleye stalked around the newly named intricacy with care.

"I was under the impression that you had some rather special knowledge regarding time displacement ..."

"Time disturbance," English corrected.

"My apologies ... I am not versed in the subject myself."

44

"Evidently . . . what was it you wished to know?" English asked.

"Whether it is within your powers to simulate a time disturbance?"

"It might be."

"Surely . . ." Lolan began the sentence, but saw the tact in not ending it.

"You mean you could . . . or rather . . . there is a faint chance that you might be able to create a time disturbance at will."

"There is more than a faint chance . . . I have already succeeded in doing so in a limited fashion. There is no reason therefore why I should not be able to do it over a much larger scene."

"Fantastic . . . right . . . off we go."

"Where to?" Lolan wished to know.

"To Colossus of course, where else. . . .?"

"Don't waste much time does he, English?"

"Is she talking to me?"

Chapter Five

"The Dwellings of Colossus" was the name given to the organic computer grown by the people of Waterspace. And as they approached, Steeleye could see, dimly, through the specially adapted viseo aboard his launch, various tall, gaunt structures looming, old and twisted, bent by the gentle ripples of Waterspace. For Colossus had no protection from the water . . . it dwelled actually in it, the currents and eddies flowing about its "circuitry". "Circuitry" was not really the word for there were none of the expected features of computer science. Indeed this place could not have looked less like a computer.

"You call this a computer?" Steeleye voiced his thoughts.

"No, I call this Colossus . . . as you see, it is not as you might imagine. These are the Dwellings of Colossus. We would do well to make our presence known shortly for Colossus is an eccentric creature."

The great launch, now winged, and sealed for travel within water, cut the drive systems and floated gently through the narrow alley ways of Colossus. To either side were buttressed balconies, hooded roofs; each bottomless, multi-windowed structure standing steady, like any township . . . any township that has been drowned by a billion tons of water.

Steeleye felt as though he had entered a world long since lost in the deepest, depths of a massive ocean. It could once have been a city, once flourishing with life, bustling with traffic . . . now a ghostly, watery grave for a thousand homes.

"Why so like a city?"

"This was her own choice . . . she grew this way, section by section over thousands of years. The resemblance to town dwellings is merely coincidence, it was not the purpose of our computer to ape other worlds."

The launch, her drive cut, drifted slowly downwards, but though they had sunk already several kilometres further, the surroundings were the same. Everywhere they were manoeuvring through tight channels, twisting with the rudder fins to slip through yet another alley way.

"What is in these . . . rooms . . . these dwellings?"

"Memories, facts, ideas, concepts, data, the food of any computer."

"But how is it stored?"

"Mostly in 4D image in the walls you might say . . . every room has an experience to give you."

"And a thousand different personalities?"

"Ah, no, the personalities live through the composite knowledge, they are not separated, at least not in fact, though Colossus is unaware that all the personalities derive from one intelligence. There is no direct being with a thousand personalities, though each does have a manifestation . . . or rather the manifestation provided for Colossus' use early in the growth is able to take on a different personality and appearance according to the changes taking place. It is more like a male manifestation than a female . . . if you can award a myth gender . . . it is called Willing."

"Willing . . . how does Willing feel about being a schizoid?"

"Willing is best described as a walking black comedy . . . not a great friend to any of us . . . and now doing the dirty work of his new master."

"Komast." Steeleye spoke.

"The same."

They remained silent as the surroundings opened out a little into a less densely constructed area. Before the launch was a patio of sorts, like the home of some noble in an ancient city, overlooking the other dwellings. And beyond the patio were more dwellings, though spread clear of where they floated.

On the right side of their direction was a particularly large plateau surrounded by domes and elaborate decorations, as though it were a throne of some sort. As they approached, Steeleye saw on the scanner that there was something or some one standing upon the upraised level.

"That is Willing." Lolan spoke. "We must stop and speak with him. Perhaps you would cover your body and mine with force and we can swim out to him."

"Very well ... English ... English?"

"Eh, oh, I'm sorry, I thought you had brought a pet animal with you or something."

"Ho ho, very funny ... please take our body bearings and remain wrapped with us ... I want a tractor beam around us and any sign of problems haul us in, right?... even teleport away out of here with us outside if you have to."

"Understood ... nevertheless ..."

"Nevertheless what ...?"

"Well, I mean ..." hesitated the computer. "All that water ... seems ... rather fishy to me." Did you ever hear a computer laugh?

"Perhaps that name wasn't so good after all," Steeleye muttered as they exited the launch.

Willing was small ... 1½ metres tall, very very thin, his face wide at the temples and narrow at the chin, the "V" shape accentuated by his eyes, which were so wide that they seemed to turn the corner of his head. The top and base lines of them were parallel, with heavy black eyebrows and the centres red. Indeed, he was not a pleasant looking character and Lolan's description of him was accurate. A black look of comedy ... as though his glance might turn you into a toad at any moment. He stood quite still and did not appear to be at all aware of their presence.

"Willing, son of Colossus, this is Lolan, come to speak with you." Lolan communicated by use of a sonic reverberator which she placed near to her throat as she moved her lips.

After a long pause Willing turned his head slowly. But his strange dark eyes did not settle upon Lolan. They passed her by and drifted with intent to the much taller, more powerful figure beside her.

Steeleye felt a small chill slide up his back and prickle the hairs on his neck.

"Hail oh Prince of the Wideways ... you are welcome in our Dwellings. ... We had thought of you many times. We count it a great privilege that you consider our humble homes a place for your mighty person."

"Willing, son of Colossus, I would count you a charlatan, were you not so powerfully surrounded, for you have already tried to remove my life from my body ... and there have been those who would now advise against such attempts, were they still living to utter the words."

The silence was a little shocked. Steeleye's direct attack, characteristic certainly, had gained him a slight advantage ... allowing that it also reduced his chances of ever getting out of this labyrinth.

"We have heard tell that Steeleye does not mince his words. ... We have heard tell that Steeleye has immortality on his side ... that the mighty Yellow who implanted the powers of the Wideways upon our present royalty of time, did so saying that 1000 years would be its term." He paused. "A handsome reward oh mighty Prince but then ... in our vaults we have heard tell of the deeds that won such an award."

"You speak like a politician Willing. ... What is it you would have of me, and of the people I have come to help?"

"We beg forgiveness, Steeleye, but it was you who came to us."

"Then, Willing the unwilling, I will state my terms."

"Be careful, Steeleye, there is unseen power here." Lolan's warning sent Steeleye's hand to his belt and a short signal was delivered to English inside the launch.

"There is one amongst your knowledge who lives under the name of Komast. This river of poison will depart the shores of Waterspace and be gone for all time."

"And if he does not?"

"Ah, a direct question from Willing's tongue, if he has one. ... If he does not, Willing, then I will see personally to

49

your disposal ... to the final deterioration and mental derangement of Colossus and to the drying up of Komast. I will ... Willing ... deal a blow ... a blow that will shake the very foundations of this watery galaxy ... a blow that you will not survive even the first reverberation ... a death blow to the living and the dead." Steeleye touched the button on his belt and English went to work.

There was a dreadful flash, a brightness that sent the computer's morbid manifestation off his podium and plunging down into hidden depths. In that flash Steeleye and Lolan were snatched back into the launch and in that flash the entire structure around them vanished, being replaced with ... empty space ... a vacuum of space which sucked the edges of the small area of Waterspace around it inwards, so that the immediate surrounds of Colossus were suddenly being dragged into the black hole. It was absolute chaos and the clean up would take Colossus some time to complete. Meantime, Steeleye and the launch cleared their way through teleportation and returned home.

One jump.

"How about that then?" shouted English as they swept away.

"I wish I could have seen it." Steeleye smiled.

"Fear not, Steeleye, I have kept a video record of the impending disaster."

"I might have guessed."

"Well, it was my first time disbursement after all."

A pause followed.

"Poor old Colossus," said Lolan.

Chapter Six

"There is only one way." Steeleye paced back and forth in front of the tree house and two small girls sat, swinging their slim legs on a branch, watching his towering figure, faintly amused.

"I am relieved to hear there is *one* . . . I had feared . . ."

"I shall have to go to Colossus myself, and lay a trap."

"A trap for whom?" Lolan was leaning against the entrance of her home, lazily, frowning.

"For Komast. But I need help."

"I will help."

"No, I need a particular kind of help . . . and there is only one who can give it. . . ."

"Who?"

"An old friend of mine . . . one I have not seen in years . . . his name is Tousle. . . . You will understand when you see him . . . he is from a race of androids who call themselves Eumigs."

"Ah, the Eumigs . . . your creators." Lolan stood up and stepped down to Steeleye's side.

"How can you get him here?"

"I can send English."

"Like a lap dog, eh?"

"Yes . . . English would bring him here."

"How long?"

"A day, two days, no more."

Zrost had moved. Since the early days when the Sylvan empire was out of the Eumig's reach – until Steeleye built the conquering bridge – they had lived alone and isolated in a far quarter of Andromeda. Earth's successor – Zrost – the world to which man emigrated and died, leaving the Eumig robots to survive, had been too far from the Empire, now Eumiga. So they moved it. Not very simple – tedious even – for it upset many of Tousle's experiments – much of his delicate planning for the future and in his own words, "Took at least 300 years off my span."

But now nearly 200 years had passed and the new home was well settled as the Eumig's domain – their headquarters for a vast and flourishing empire. But you wouldn't have known it to look at the place.

Take a typical scene – a very green scene as like of Zrost. Nothing had really changed much – because the Eumigs did not deteriorate very often and only eight new ones had been constructed in 200 years. The atmosphere was artificial so it did not matter at all where the planet was in space. On the surface were carefully planned and divided "fields". This particular scene is the one Tousle enjoyed from his laboratory. The building, low built and the only one in that sector, was on a slight hill, its shape moulding with the hill, the floor dug into the earth, the roof curved. On either side was a long, flat roadway, very narrow, for use by the ground cars which occasionally brought materials to the labs. Mostly though, the road was there because Tousle liked it. In the middle distance was a tall-spired church – "Because I like churches," transported from Earth as a kind of monument. And on the distant hill top, echoing Tousle's labs, were Hamgar's labs – Steeleye's creator – the other creature Scientist.

No big sky scrapers. No belching vehicles.

The eumigs preffered the coolness of open spaces and the calm of less violated structures. They had lived with man and learnt from Man largely what not to do with their planet. It had taken 1600 years to erase the effects of Man on Zrost. Now it was peaceful. Completely controlled by machines, it was efficient and the air was clean.

"Clean air prolongs active life – remember that PAL," Tousle would say. One thing you would find with this robot – he had such a memory, like you would not believe – he remembered the craziest things.

On this particular day, the air was as clean as ever – but with the humidity turned up a little high.

"What is wrong with the humidity levels, Control?" Tousle spoke internally on the TI channels which connected all the Eumigs and their computers. TI is Telephathic Insinuation – you might call it ESP.

The computer replied, "On the blink, Tousle."

"Not entirely the answer I would expect from an Exon computer, but still. Get it off the blink then – it's overdewing the vegetation. We'll have an early crop, or some such."

"Steeleye's launch has just entered Andromeda ... it is headed here, but he is not aboard – Timion instructed me to advise you."

"Thank you ... I will speak with the computer aboard. Please establish contact, and don't forget the humidity levels – or I'll stop your Positonic for the week."

"You may speak now." The computer belched.

"Steeleye computer, 345/uy, where is your master?"

"I have a name now, Tousle." The computer spoke with a definite arrogance, even over several light years.

"A name? What do you mean?"

"Lolan gave me a name Tousle. It is English. Perhaps you would address me as such in future."

"What is it with you guys ... first I get a half-wit grand computer who can't get the waterworks right, then some chunk of metal not fit to be an auto-pilot is giving *me* orders. I thought we'd got the better of you lot by now. Listen ... you are nearly five light years distant and the power you are using up to tell me your name is costing Zrost approximately 8,000 credits per hour. I would be most grateful if you would reserve the formalities for your imminent arrival which I time at approximately 23.45."

"Correct, Tousle. I will teleport at once."

"I should bloody well think so too."

"What took you so long?" English had executed a jump to make any Olympic teleporter proud ... five light years in three minutes and 14 seconds ... only one jump through space/time.

53

"My apologies Tousle, but I was uncertain of the co-ordinates for the areas around Tarnmood 3."

"Excuses, excuses ... Now where is Steeleye?"

"He is in Waterspace, Tousle ..."

"Waterspace? Waterspace ... that rings a bell ... Waterspace ... a moment, I must refer to ..."

"There is no need, Tousle. Steeleye has asked urgently that you board my launch and allow me to take you there."

"Why is he not come himself? Or need I ask ... I suppose he's saving some maiden in distress. ..."

"That would be a fairly accurate assessment."

"And her name is Lolan?"

"Correct again."

"English did you say?"

"Yes."

"Hm, appropriate enough I suppose ... shows a certain degree of intelligence. ... Very well, wait a ten minute and I will be ready to go. ... Restock with food and any preparations Steeleye has not been able to acquire in the past three years. ... Take some of his favourite. ... That stuff, what's it called?"

"Crom, Tousle."

"Yes, crom. Dreadful filth. Who on Zrost introduced him to such muck. I can't imagine ..."

"I believe it was ..."

"Just prepare for take off in 9.4 minutes."

"Yes, Tousle."

"English ..." Tousle departed the labs and made for Timion's chambers.

Lolan's first impression of the Android she had heard so much about was that from a space launch adapted for the size and shape of the massive Steeleye, Tousle had to stoop to exit.

He was gigantic ... more than 3 metres in height, his body like an athlete who has done a season on top of a mountain with weights.

The shoulders were wider than wide, with bulges at each end and tense powerful sinews across the front collar. The chest front bulged, a little like a matronly bosom and the joints in places were slightly exposed. The robot was male in general appearance, but there was a smooth, sleek curve away between the great massive legs. The stomach area was covered in shadow controls, the purpose of which Lolan could not guess. Otherwise all control and adjustment must have been under internal directions.

The face was near human, the eyes, both like the one steel eye in Steeleye's face; red-hued, metallic shining and bold.

His movements were loping . . . wide steps that seemed to reflect a generous, untroubled nature . . . if nature could be applied to a mechanical, electronic instrument. How strange . . . it had only just occurred to Lolan that he was in fact a robotic mechanisation, not living at all. Indeed he was the only thing within Waterspace at this moment, other than English, that was not alive.

Nevertheless, he seemed too pleasant to admonish for that.

"You are Lolan. . . . My name is Tousle. . . . Please excuse me if I greet my friend. I have not seen him for almost three years."

They embraced, Tousle lifting Steeleye's great body from the ground as he gripped him about the chest.

Steeleye gasped for breath as he was deposited back on firm ground.

"You have grown no weaker, Tousle."

"You are still puny . . ."

Steeleye laughed and slapped Tousle with an enormous clout, powerful enough to fell a tree. Tousle jerked slightly forward, turning to look at Steeleye. The thin lips about the mouth widened in the Eumig simulated smile.

"Now, Lolan, what troubles can this oaf not sort out for you that he needs the help of a Eumig?"

Lolan was amazed by this awesome creature . . . she stood before one of the most notorious personalities in the Universe. Here was a leader, indeed, second in command of the mighty and ancient Sylvan Empire, now Eumiga, a robot . . . the only robot ever to build a living creature, and he was concentrating upon her.

"No, you are not strictly correct in that assumption Lolan ... Steeleye was not built by me at all ... he was built by my associate Hamgar ... I built Chaos."

"You read my thoughts? And who is Chaos?"

"Yes, forgive me ... I will not insult you by encroaching upon your thoughts again ... and Chaos is a woman ... a most beautiful woman ... as beautiful indeed as you are."

"You are kind ... why is she not with you, Steeleye?"

"Because the journeys I have made in the last years were suitable only for one ... only for me. ... Chaos remained on Zrost."

"Well, some of the time on Zrost ... she has been doing her own adventuring in your absence."

Steeleye raised an eyebrow.

"Would you expect anything less in so long a time?" Lolan queried.

Steeleye smiled.

There was a silent pause as they made their way along the beach.

"Have you children, Steeleye?"

"Yes, Lolan ... Chaos has given birth to eight children and there are others by others to us both ... I believe that the extent of Man is now some thirty thousand."

"Thirty thousand. ... That is a great many ... surely."

"I am 185 years old Lolan. ... It is surprising there are not more than thirty thousand."

"All descended from you or Chaos ..."

"Or both ..." Tousle added.

"No ... all descended from Hamgar and Tousle." Steeleye smiled at Tousle. "Strange bedfellows."

Tousle entered the dwelling first.

INTER-DEPART-MENTAL MEMORANDUM TO ALL MENTALITIES

It–should–be–noted–that–there–has–been–a–further–arrival–within–the–hallowed–portals–of–Waterspace——One–Tousle–a–most–notable–Eumig. It–is–proposed–that–Komast–be–informed–of–this–development–at–once.

INTER-DEPART-MENTAL MEMORANDUM FROM C67 TO ALL DEPARTS

That–means–we'll–have–to–tell–him–about–the–cock-up–we–made–not–so–long–ago–dum–dum. Doesn't–it–eh–eh?

INTER-DEPARTMENTAL REPLY FROM CENTRAL TO C67

What–choice–do–we–have–clever–dicky–trickery? You–tell–us–and–we'll–do–it.

INTER-DEPART-MENTAL REPLY FROM C67 TO ALL

Send–down–the–Mecha-Tanks–right–now–and–blow–the–lot-to-kingdom-went.

INTER-DEPART REPLY

Oh–clever–thinking–and–what–kind–of–mess–do–you–think–those–two–big–hoods–would–make–of–half–a–dozen–Mecha-Tanks–in–seconds–flat–I–tell–you–what–kind–of–a–nut–are–you–anyway?

INTER-PERSONALITY-DEFECTUALITY MEMO

If–we–could–just–get–him–here–then–we'd–show–'em–wouldn't–we?

MENTAL DEPART AGREEMENT

If–we–could–just–. . .

"I must stay here on my island . . ." Lolan twisted a small fallen leaf in her hands, her head down.

"They might attack while we're gone though . . . you can afford to lose the others, but they can't afford to lose you . . ."

57

Steeleye tried to persuade her to come with them.

"And if you get caught by Colossus, which you will ... then where would I be?"

"She is right, Steeleye. Lolan must stay here, but we can leave your launch ... er English ... with a little auto-priming that launch can do a fox trot around those Mecha-Tanks."

"Very well. I will prepare English." Steeleye walked to the launch.

There was a moment's silence before Lolan turned to Tousle.

"You will look after him? He is a good creature. He cares. Not many care outside our worlds."

"I will care for him ... I have done so many times before ... and we Eumigs are difficult to harm."

Lolan sat silently beside Tousle. She felt overawed by his size still and the foreignness of his electronics. How could something appear to be so alive ... and yet have nothing to commend it to life whatever? It seemed obscene to her. As though a basic law of nature had been broken and this travesty, however attractive and lovable he was, constantly forced his existence upon life. Like a blunt weapon pushing up the unyielding surface of the environment, trying to etch its own way, but never able to join, only straining against too powerful a source. She turned to look upon his head, sideways to hers, and she saw a nobility that was never grown from death.

"Do you ponder on our strangeness, Lolan?"

"You've been reading my thoughts again," she jibed, half hurt that he should break his word.

"No, I have terminated any TI reception. But it is not hard to deduce your feelings from logical patterns."

"You see ... you are so alive ... you can feel. You can at least understand feelings. Why should I worry that you do not live?"

"Because everything around you, for 400 years has been alive. Every thought in your head, every atom about your body is as alive as you. How could you readily accept a hand-built, electronic machine like myself? Why should I

58

wish to live? That is something you have not considered. If I were to be alive I would have to find the most elaborate way of extending my life for as long as a million years."

"Is that your potential span?"

"It is. You see ... I do not believe in life. I regard it as yet another method ... another system of observing what occurs around it. I can observe such occurrences better, longer, quicker. I can absorb and record such surroundings more rapidly and with greater accuracy and with more interrelation than any living creature could. My body is stronger, more agile, more content, more in tune, fitter, than any living body can possibly be. My brain, which I carry here in my chest, is eight times the size of Steeleye's, three thousand times faster in every way, able to absorb as many as sixty different stimuli at the same moment, more sensitive to smell, taste, touch, pain, anger or any emotional or physical response you care to name. I can see an insect four kilometres away, and I can hear a honey bee buzzing at eight kilometres. I read minds like you read video tapes and I carry thirty different defence weapons. Why should I wish also to live?"

Lolan smiled. "You're just a dirty great thug, aren't you?"

"Thug?" Tousle was hurt. "Why do you call me that? I would not harm a fly."

"No, of course not ... it was only meant as an endearment. I understand now why Steeleye loves you so much ..."

Tousle felt a little like a child, patted on the head by a wise old parent.

"And I understand why Steeleye is so eager to help you ... and your people."

Lolan smiled at him once more and then stood, wrapping her arms about Steeleye's strong waist as he returned to the menage.

"Tousle has been telling me of how he longs for life ... be sure that he comes back in one piece then perhaps I might be able to give him a small gift."

Tousle frowned, the strange, quietly implied truth upsetting his own delicately balanced emotional construction.

59

"Come Tousle, we must leave. English will react automatically to any attack. You need have no fear. Just get your people into their homes, or the water, and he will do the rest."

"That is comforting, Steeleye. Thank you ... now, beware, both of you, for yourselves.... You are dear to us too."

Chapter Seven

Lolan stood on the waterside watching them disappear across to the departure rocks. She waited, all the time moving her long-fingered hands in the manner of her people, sending fortune and love with them. She turned when they were out of sight and with her hands cupped to her mouth she gave a long, low call, her voice waving up and down, sliding through all the ranges.

She sat then upon the ground, waiting.

Within moments of the call came a winged creature, speeding towards her. As it came closer, Lolan could distinguish who had responded. It was Peatre, one of the few winged people upon Pensil. Peatre often carried Lolan to other parts of the planet, and now she was summoned for a special journey. The girl was tall, naked and fine skinned, with no mark upon her body, every centimetre quite smooth. Her small breasts were perfect and her legs strong and muscular. She had huge wings at her back and long, long thin tentacles that stretched, two from either side of her body. On her head were two further small feelers.

Peatre was blind ... all the winged people were blind, and moved by radar. The small tentacles on her head were sensitive scanners and she could manoeuvre through far more complex places than anyone with eyes. Her radar system would detect movement over many kilometres. Her face was fresh and warm, with pink cheeks and red lips. Her eyes were quite blue, and they had no pupils and no iris, simply a bright stark blueness which covered the whole ball of each eye, giving her a weird appearance. Though when she smiled at Lolan her beauty was startling.

"Peatre, thank you. . . . Will you carry me to Mysemnia?"

"Mysemnia? Do you go to see her?" The round young face looked startled but not fearful of Lolan's plans.

"Of course. I have to speak with her."

"Then I will take you. Come, climb on my back."

The journey was a long one, covering several hundred kilometres and much of it over water. Near to the Castle of Mysemnia were few islands and a feeling of bleakness covered the castle itself.

Mysemnia was the oldest of the people on Pensil and lived alone in the castle where she had little contact with others. She had isolated herself there now for many years and only on occasion did she speak to visitors. Very often she would turn them away without reason. But Lolan was one of her daughters and Mysemnia would not turn her away, for she held great love for her and welcomed her visits.

The castle was a tree; an enormous tree that grew eight hundred metres from the ground and measured a 100 metres across. It had many entrances and exists, many tunnels and throughways and drawn from the ground to its base and round the whole width ran a winding roadway. The tree was pure white and at its top were the characteristic natural houses, full of windows and doors that made it look like a mushroom outcrop.

Lolan was set down by Peatre half-way up the path.

"I will wait here for you, Lolan, and carry you back again when you leave your mother."

"Thank you, Peatre." And Lolan began to climb the long road.

As she drew closer, a figure appeared at the entrance which ended the road. It was Mysemnia. Her gaunt frame glittered with the ostentatious clothing she wore, the gown shining with a strange light – the light of her immortal soul. Her hair was longer than her body and the face was long too.

"Come Lolan, what do you need of your tired mother?"

"I would talk of Steeleye, Mysemnia ... I have an uneasiness within me."

"Do you think the right hand knows what all the other hands are doing?" Tousle addressed the query to Steeleye across a narrow chasm. Tousle stood on one balcony of

Colossus' many "rooms" while Steeleye stood on another. Then they changed to another sector.

"I would imagine that we are expected, indeed, that we are smack in the middle of a very simple trap. . . . Wouldn't you?"

And so they switched again. Now Steeleye stood on the roof of a growth that stuck out like an elongated neck poking from a distorted body. Tousle was a few metres away on a small podium that appeared barely strong enough to carry the 1200 kilos standing upon it.

"I think it most likely, Steeleye, most likely. And . . ." They switched again, each move performed with maximum bravado, teleporting a few metres about the Dwellings. ". . . what do you propose we should do about it, the trap I mean?"

"Show of power?"

"Good enough . . . you start, I'll follow."

Steeleye executed a dive from the level where he stood and like a monster Peter Pan he swerved in and out of the Dwellings, blasting with his eye, knocking and toppling structures in every direction. The movements were so swift that he could arrive three destructions away before the first had fallen.

Tousle meanwhile sent a charge of high voltage through his feet and gradually broke down the tissues of Colossus below them.

Eventually the podium collapsed and Tousle remained standing in mid air. He fired both his eyes ahead of him and smacked a whole dwelling from its promontory.

As he was about to set off to another part of the immediate area, a TI message came across from Steeleye.

"I think we've got company."

Tousle looked up, relieved that the destruction perhaps now could be directed rather than random.

The movement of the water swished gently about Tousle's head as he looked around for the enemy. When he saw it, there was little time to study. It was obviously the computer's manifestation again. A small creature, wizened and old.

63

"Get out," it said and without a moment to answer, Tousle found himself out. And next to him, like an inebriate ejected from a drinking house, tumbled Steeleye, rolling through empty space. No water. They really had been kicked out. Just like that.

"Well, that was clever, wasn't it?" Steeleye remarked as he regained his dignity and moved to within reach of the Eumig.

"I feel a little red faced. . . . We appear to be dealing with more than we had reckoned on."

"Yes . . . well . . . where are we?"

"Not far from my entry point. Unless I am mistaken there is a lighthouse somewhere hereabouts."

"A lighthouse?"

"Yes, a beacon, the part of Colossus which shows above the water . . . a kind of periscope if you like. It's very large and distinctive. You can't miss it, as they say."

"Do they? Well, then, find it Tousle, find it."

"There is one problem."

"Oh?" Steeleye shuffled a little, irritated at being ejected so easily, wishing to get back into the fray.

"If we find the periscope, we may well find Komast at the same time. It is the point whereby he hopes to enter . . . or so English has deduced."

"Chatting to you on the way here, was he?"

"Yes, the name has done something for him. So what do you think? Do you feel ready after that exit, to meet Komast?"

"Hm, I don't know about you but I feel a little like a fighter with short arms. Perhaps we should take the back entrance and walk a little more quietly."

"Very well . . . just one point. You are satisfied that Lolan is . . . to be trusted . . . ?"

"I hadn't thought about it . . . why?"

"Well, there are inconsistencies . . . but no matter . . . if there is doubt in you, it can wait for the moment. Come, let's get to this periscope."

As Tousle had imagined, there was a tall structure that rose from the water of Waterspace like a submarine's periscope, though more elaborate. Its long scraggy neck rose out of the slightly moving water like a stretched limb, pulling away from the body beneath the water. The head was rounded, unevenly pitted with empty holes, and domed at the curving lid with a shaggy baldness, no shields, or guarding device, no visible weaponry. Steeleye and Tousle moved closer expecting something to be slung at them, but it didn't come and soon they were within gravitational spitting distance.

"Well ... they don't seem to care about us, do they?" Steeleye ventured closer, until he was able to touch the outside surface.

"Any impulse?" Tousle had expected Steeleye's body to be flung away by some violent shock.

"Nothing. Placid as a Teegerhog."

"O.K. Let's go." They both climbed in through the nearest hole, neutralising the fine force field which kept the vacuum of space in its place. They were in an air lock and once the tiny chamber had been filled they were able to move into the entrance.

"Now what?" Tousle asked uncharacteristically.

"We'd better have a look around ... I don't understand this, this deadness. As though no-one had been hereabouts for years. Or they've set another trap."

The inside of the periscope was falling to pieces. Great vaulted rooms lead through doorless entrances to more rooms, each one larger.

Because of the organic structure of Colossus, nothing was ordered, or designed, nothing in the least consistent. Each room had a different shape, and now it seemed that none had any purpose at all. The ceilings were flaking and the floors were covered in the debris of fallen rubble. The rooms looked like they had a bad case of dandruff.

They continued downwards and inwards towards the guts of the computer. But the chambers continued empty. Like an abandoned mansion where the previous inhabitants only ever occupied one wing. The floors were covered in this flaking debris and the walls showed total neglect.

"You could go mad here with a do-it-yourself-manual."

"A what?" Steeleye did not turn to face his friend.

"Never mind. I'm picking up movement somewhere not far below."

"What sort of movement?" They drew closer together instinctively.

"Can't say exactly, something intelligent, though of doubtful origin, moving about ... I'm afraid it's only my vibratory pads that are picking it up. I have no sensory life readings. Whatever it is, it's not exactly alive. But it's thumping about anyway."

"Well, let's get closer. There's nothing here."

They moved towards the vibrations until, after another four large chambers, they entered one without an exit doorway. They were able to enter it but no hole would let them out in any other direction.

"Dead end," Steeleye noted, usefully.

"This is where the vibrations are coming from, on the other side of that wall."

"Maybe we picked the wrong route."

"There was no alternative. We've come the only way we could."

They stood in the middle of the room, looking about at the surfaces. There were no breaks or adhesions, nothing to suggest that anything had passed that way before. But, as Tousle began to approach the opposite wall, intending to search for some kind of "matter phaser", there was a small, almost tentative clicking sound ... a sort of ... "Ticker-ticker-ticker". Tousle took off. His body moved like a Hopper-copter, one impulse and he was standing beside Steeleye on the other side of the room, every reactor in his massive frame tensed for defence. But it was not to be that simple. The wall, or half of it, up to around 4 metres, faded to nothing and on the other side was a tall, vaulted and elegant room. Steeleye's general impression, as the wall drew aside, was that the room was very green, all the shades, the floor covering and the chairs ... chairs?? There were real, old fashioned chairs scattered about the room. Behind them a massive window, again in an ancient style, with glass framed sashes. On the "outside" of the window was a garden, huge and beautifully tended, with massive trees, flowers and grass. There was even a sky above it and a roadway that meandered out of sight.

Taking all this in, Steeleye almost missed the most important feature; a long-faced, sad-looking Man sitting in the chair before the window, his legs close together, the feet drawn up under the chair and his hands placed neatly on his lap. He wore a beard and spectacles, a long coat and a tie. Steeleye had seen pictures of such dress, but they related to times way before even the arrival of Man on Zrost. This had to be a hoax ... Steeleye chanced his arm.

"Good day, Willing."

"You are mistaken, sir. My name is Abelard, please enter. ... You may bring your ... er ... machine with you." The description was directed at Tousle, who blinked in astonishment at what was, after all, only accurate.

"Sit down, I'm sure you can both squeeze into the chairs. They were not exactly built for you, but nevertheless ..."

The words trailed off as though he were preoccupied by something else outside their vision. Steeleye and Tousle sat, speechless.

Abelard spoke again: "I would be most interested to know gentlemen from where you have come and ... er ... where you are intending to go."

Steeleye looked behind him and saw that where they had entered there was a plain wall, covered in pictures, framed paintings and designs. No door, or window.

"Perhaps it would be better if you were to tell us where we are because I'm afraid we appear to have been deflected from our direction."

"I see, well that should be simple enough. ... You have found yourself in the home of Abelard Showman of whom no doubt you have some slight knowledge."

Steeleye looked at Tousle and Tousle looked at Steeleye. They both returned to look at Mr. Showman and nodded that they did not even have a slight knowledge of him. He looked very disappointed, not to say slightly put out.

"I'm afraid Abelard Showman that your name does not help us very much for you see, we are not simply lost in

67

your neighbourhood, but lost also as to the position of your planet both in space and time."

"Ah ... oooooooooH." The first was an understanding, the second, a shock. "You mean you're from another planet?"

"Yes, that is correct."

"And another time also?"

"Right again." Tousle added, and Abelard looked at him, regarding the giant with a mixture of distaste and disbelief.

"In that case I fear that my good intentions are quite wasted, for I do not possess either a space ship or a time machine ..."

Steeleye and Tousle looked at one another again and shrugged. When they returned their eyes to Abelard he was standing, though neither had seen him get up, looking out of the window at his garden.

"Have you gardens on your planet, gentlemen?"

"After a fashion, though used only for vegetation." Tousle spoke.

"May I ask, sir, without wishing in any way to insult you, of what race of man you stem from?" His tone was one of genuine enquiry.

"I am a Eumig, and I stem from the scientific genius of Man, now a dead race ..." Tousle's brain was ticking over ... how would this fellow know of Man? ...

"So I was right in supposing that you are made from ... er ... forgive me ... I mean no disrespect ... artificial materials."

"That depends upon the terms of reference ... if you will tell me what you regard as genuine, I will tell you whether the materials which form my body are artificial."

"Oh ... oh ... oh dear ... I have insulted you. I was afraid that I might. ... Please ... I was only ..." Abelard was really concerned, though it was misplaced for Tousle felt no insult. Indeed he actually "felt" nothing at all.

"Perhaps you would now tell us the name of your own world ... Abelard?" Tousle asked casually.

"Oh, haven't I done so? This is Earth of course ... Earth,

68

1906 ... er ... A.D." There was a pause, as Steeleye and Tousle both blinked and questioned each other over the TI wires, but there were no answers.

"Perhaps I might suggest a walk in the garden, you are not looking very well, sir...." Abelard addressed himself to Steeleye. He turned and opened the only door in the room and led them outside.

The garden was huge, stretching away for several hundred metres and on one side was a great big maze.

"Have you ever seen a maze, gentlemen? Forgive me, I am presuming that you are not from Earth."

"You are correct, though we are fully conversant with the history of Earth." Tousle looked down at the tiny fellow between them.

"The whole of Earth's history?"

"Yes."

"You mean, Earth ... one day ... will cease to exist?"

"No, it will not cease to exist. At least, not for a few million centuries, but it will lose its first civilisation quite soon."

"Soon?" Abelard seemed genuinely distressed. "You mean even in my life time?"

"No, I mean during the 25th century."

"Oh, well, that is hardly soon."

"In galactic terms, Abelard, it is tomorrow."

Abelard nodded, his eyebrows raised in a gesture of awe.

They proceeded towards the maze and stopped at its entrance.

"Come, let us take our courage in our hands and see where we end up."

The hedges of the maze were five metres tall so that not even Tousle could see over them, except of course by a short rocket boost. They began to walk between the hedges and Abelard chattered away inquisitively.

"Of course I do have a considerable knowledge of astronomy, for instance I am aware of the position of the heavens, indeed were it presently dark I could point out to

69

you the whereabouts of some thirty different heavenly bodies. A fair proportion, don't you think?"

"Very commendable Abelard, and where did you learn such extensive knowledge?"

Tousle remained respectful, for he had no tongue to cheek.

"Oh, there is much literature on the subject these days, you see gentlemen, an Austrian has recently written some remarkable theories about time and space and the like."

"Mr. Albert Einstein, you mean?" Steeleye asked.

"Oh you know of him? Yes, that is correct. I'm sure his discoveries will have an effect for a while. No doubt though, they will be found to be incorrect sooner or later ... but for the time being, so to speak the stars are rather popular. People are bored you know, they need a war or two to keep them happy."

Tousle and Steeleye remained non-committal, both on the subjects of Einstein's theory of relativity and the war that was soon to hit the world. They approached the maze, the little man in the middle constantly stroking the pointed beard upon his chin, his long thin arms otherwise swinging loosely at his side. Steeleye found himself forgetting their unexpected arrival and concentrating on the opportunity it presented.

He sniffed the air and began to indulge a long wish, yet unfulfilled, to return to Earth and live a few years in seclusion there.

"I ... um, presume sir, that you are ... not akin to our own race ... that you have special characteristics that do not occur shall we say, in the race of Man?" Abelard was fascinated by Tousle, but unwilling to insult the giant.

"I am what will be known on your world as an Android ... a sort of advanced robot. My construction is purely electronic, I have no life as such within me, but I function somewhat similarly to a man."

"He can remember anything ... anything you like ... for example, I'm sure he could tell you all the famous names of people born this year on Earth and what they will be known for."

70

Steeleye patted Tousle on the back, smiling at him.

They continued their journey in the maze, neither realising exactly why they were there, and neither thinking even for a moment that there could be any danger.

"How fascinating. Do tell me, who is born this year. . . . Who will be famous? What about David Peebottom, next door?"

"No, that is not a name I have on my records, though of course there could be a gap. . . . As far as I can be aware . . . during the course of the year 1906 on Earth, Samuel Beckett was born . . . er . . . what is the date today?"

"16th February."

"Ah, Samuel Beckett is to be born on the 15th April. . . . He will be one of the world's most celebrated playwrights. Then there is Hugh Gaitskell born on April 9th this year . . . he becomes leader of the Labour party in the 1950s I believe. . . ."

"The what party?"

"The Labour . . . oh, I believe you call it now the Socialist party."

"Ah, yes. . . . Oh dear, do you mean that the communists get in . . . ?"

"Not for a little while yet, no."

"Oh, good, please go on, who else . . . ?"

"Henrik Ibsen will die on May 23rd this year and on September 25th Dmitri Shostakovich will be born . . . one day to be a great composer."

"You should pop over to his parents and tell them they are to have a boy. . . . I'm sure they'd be thrilled to know of his future."

The maze was very high, and not so wide and Steeleye, without allowing the sensation much credence, began to feel a little "hedged in". They continued to walk.

Every so often they would make a turn. Steeleye comforted himself in the knowledge that Tousle's retentive brain would be taking a detailed record of their direction.

"There is one small question I would ask of you, Abelard." Tousle ventured.

"Yes, of course, anything sir."

"Have you walked inside this maze before?"

"Never, no, not to my knowledge, and I'm not in the habit of sleep walking."

"You live in this house, with these gardens and yet you have never walked in the maze?"

"Oh, did I say I lived in the house? . . . No, I don't think I did, because I don't. – No indeed, I must say I wish I did. The place is rather pleasant, isn't it? Yes, er, no rather, I don't live here. It is merely a visitor to me."

"A visitor *to you*? The house and garden are visitors *to* you?"

"That is correct gentlemen. . . . However I have now returned the house to its original owners but the maze remains. . . . Oh, and I sent back the sky too. Not really a very nice sky anyway . . . I had rather hoped for a dark starry one, always fancied myself as an astronomer, you know, but there wasn't one around the place at the time. . . . Still you can't have everything. . . . Good day gentlemen, happy hunting. I think you'll find a number of things to your interest . . . I mean how often do you get the chance to walk around a multi-personality computered maze in your life . . . te . . . he . . . ticker-ticker."

And Abelard Showman, alias Willing, alias The Dwellings of Colossus was gone, leaving the two intrepids somewhat duped.

Chapter Eight

The tops of the hedgerows were sealed. No attempts to rise above it all were in the least successful. They retraced their steps to the beginning, where there should have been an entrance but there was only a dead end.

And attached to the hedge was a large sign, a white piece of card, with the very words on it: "DEAD END".

It mocked them, as they stood, ineptly beneath.

It was saying between those two words, "This is Steeleye and Tousle, two giants of the Universe, stuck in a lousy maze."

They both sat down, because there seemed little point in doing anything else.

"There must be a sensible way out of this," Tousle suggested.

"Huh, mazes are jokes. Nobody ever gets out of a maze unless there's a guy who can climb up on a platform and wave his arms. In movies people never get out of mazes, so how can two giants of the Universe stuck in a lousy maze ever expect to get out. .... No, I reckon we're here for a million years or so."

"Don't be foolish, Steeleye, there is always a logical way out of everything."

"Well, you lost me. I think I'll just have a quick snooze."

Whereupon Steeleye lay down and closed his human eye. When he opened it again Tousle had gone.

"Tousle?" Steeleye spoke. No-one answered. "Tousle?" Again silence.

Steeleye stood up and walked to the next turn. Tousle wasn't there

"Stupid bloody robot. Tousle?"

Nothing. "Where the hell are you Tousle? What's the

idea going off like this when I'm having a quick nap, Tousle?" No sound.

He was walking backwards towards another turn in the maze and as he moved into it, he heard a sound. It was midway between a grunt and a scream, muffed. He turned with characteristic speed and some ten metres distant at the other end of that sector, stood a most hideous creature. It was stringy and very thin – like an undernourished refugee – each joint close enough to the surface for a pin prick to expose the bone. The hands were strung together like worry beads. The back was bent and curved as though it carried a huge weight and the eyes shifted constantly, always wary, uncertain and burdened. A crook looking for a cop.

The head was so skinny, a wig would slide off and the scraggy bird-like neck waited unwillingly for the farmer's hatchet – the adam's apple hit him under the chin every so often.

Everything was bare flesh, livid with pock marks, each one at least an inch in diameter. The marks oozed and spat a very unpleasant pus which the creature was forced to shake from its ghastly head every few moments.

It growled as though in considerable pain and discomfort and advanced towards Steeleye in a manner that could only suggest similar growths between its legs.

It groaned with a sort of fake horror, as though its task was not altogether a happy one. Its face was really very unpleasant, with warts and gashes, a kind of volcanic planatary body, the various coloured or discoloured poisons oozing copiously from every crater.

"Grrrrrrrrrawrwrrrrrah." It said. And took three further, most painful steps towards Steeleye, who stood uncertain whether to laugh or cry.

"Grawwwwwwwwwhhhrrarrraraw – arrgh – argh – – orhhhhhhh." Came the next cry, the steps less certain with every half metre. Then it looked up at Steeleye for the first time. He was a full metre taller and manifestly unimpressed.

"Hello." He said, quite friendly, really. Whether the monster understood the one word sentiment was uncertain from its reaction. The head tilted as far as it could without cracking the brittle bones, and a kind of dubious dog look came over the hanging features. It blinked several times and then took an unconscious step backwards, wobbled on its diseased legs and sat with a great thump on its poxy bum. Steeleye looked down upon this extraordinary creature, with a deep frown on his brow. Somehow he could not imagine this to be a hoax, though it was conceivable that upon his closer arrival, it might leap dextrously into the air and sting him with some deadly poison. But that would hardly be effective through the almost metal plate of his force shield, now firmly erected.

So Steeleye did advance closer, and sat down in front of the monster, crossed his legs and addressed himself to the task.

Sitting exactly where it had landed, the pathetic creature cried, the tears running the devious and mottled route of its face. A sad thing, this monster.

"Do you know anything about mazes, or organic computers?" Steeleye asked hopefully. The monster nodded that it did.

"Do you know a way out of here?"

The answer was again an affirmative nod.

"Then what in Komast's name are you doing here?" At the mention of Komast the monster shrank back violently and the shrouded and styed eyes almost popped like the surrounding pus factories.

"Did he send you here, after me?"

A vigorous nod sent a wet dog-shake spray of many colours across the ground between them.

"Are you one of Colossus' personalities?"

Yes, he was, and evidently a most unwilling one.

The pathetic creature then began an elaborate sign language, waving its arms about in a totally incoherent fashion. It seemed desperately to be attempting speech, without success.

"Slow down, slow down. Start again, what are you trying to tell me?"

Now began the process in slower motion indicating to

75

Steeleye that Tousle had been removed to the computer's laboratories for closer examination, that there was a simple way back there and that if Steeleye did not get a move on he might easily find his mate in a million little pieces. He ended by gesturing that he had meant no harm and that really Colossus wasn't such a bad guy. Just watch out for Komast who was rotten through.

"O.K. buddy, let's go." Steeleye stood, but the monster remained grounded.

"What's the matter, monster?"

It indicated the hideousness of its body with a strangely poetic stroke of its riddled hands. The gesture was followed by a grimace that gave ugliness to ugliness, and it spat at its own feet.

"Did you get all that mess from your personality or from Komast?"

The creature indicated the former. And then, low and behold it spoke, for the first time. "I am the guilt of The Dwellings. I carry the sores of its past." And the voice rumbled out like a glorious symphony of deep, deep bubbles. It was the most fascinating and rapturous voice Steeleye had ever encountered. He stood before it as it spoke and smiled, for there was no other reaction in his mind.

"My house amongst Colossus is the garbage of deceit, the dung heap where she casts her debris. I carry the greatest weight of all our persons."

"Why did you not speak before, monster? Your voice heals the sores on your body."

"If you were carrying ten thousand years of guilt and deception, you would have trouble getting it out."

"Yes, I suppose that is true. So you must be suffering right now, with Komast around." The word again produced a convulsion of horror within the broken frame of the monster and for several moments it was unable to speak. Finally, after enormous physical effort the words stuttered forth.

"K-K-K-K-K-K-Komast uses me .... h-h-h-he uses me for his dirty work a-a-a-and then Colossus lumbers m-m-me with the guilt of my acts."

"But surely there must be a deceiver too. I mean, if you carry the guilt, there must be another personality that perpetrates it."

"Oh, yes, he's got her well occupied."

"Oh, that one's a she, is it?"

"Oh, we're all she's. I'm she too. Don't be d-d-d-deceived by my voice, that is simply a result of too much Hypletherias."

"What is Hypletherias?"

"A sort of d-d-drug . . ."

"What for a heavy guilt complex?"

"Y-y-y-yes, Colossus takes it through her inward nervous s-s-system and I get it . . . and it affects my voice . . . d-d-d-don't ask me why."

"I won't. I think your voice is beautiful."

"Do you?" The monster's face was transformed, from its hideous visage of excretion to an amazing parody of delight and embarrassment

At last the female was through. Steeleye had tamed the mad dog . . . rather easily made a friend.

"What is your name, monster?"

"I am C456, but they call me Culp." Culp sagged visibly.

"Well, Culp, my old friend, let's see if we can't help each other. You show me the way out of this place and I'll try and get rid of King Komast."

Culp raised a hand to touch Steeleye and retracted it, her face shadowing over and then retreating to resignation.

Steeleye followed the tortured and dragging steps through the maze until they reached an opening that emptied the hedged air into nowhere. Again, the glorious rumbling voice gestured to Steeleye that he would be safe to follow.

"Come, Steeleye, we have to fly a little . . . I prefer it myself, it hurts less." There was much suffering in those words and Steeleye watched Culp lift off the sparkling grass and float through nothingness, slowly downwards. Steeleye followed likewise. The journey took a few moments and Steeleye watched as Culp sadly landed upon the hard ground. There was no sign of where they were until Steeleye too had come down, then quite suddenly, the walls and ceiling of Colossus' inside surrounded them. They were back in Waterspace, inside the organic computer. Strangely, Steeleye felt a great sense of relief.

"Quickly, we may be in time to save Tousle."

"I would not bet that Tousle is in need of saving."

"There are many to fight against, Steeleye...."

"Indeed? We shall see."

Culp touched a control on the wall of the chamber they occupied and a screen replaced it.

"This is a video of the events taking place in the chamber where Tousle was taken. It is one of the largest chambers in the computer, and in a moment we should see what is happening."

The picture blurred into view and all hell had broken loose in that chamber. Tousle stood at the centre of the most fantastic fray. There were at least forty creatures of varying size and shape either rushing at him, being thrown back by him or lying battered in the various corners. Tousle was not evidently strained, his eyes were blazing, his vast shoulders swinging like a pair of massive windmills, as he strode about the chamber dispatching the attackers one after another. Each time one fell dead another would come from the entrance and take its place. But Tousle was quite tireless. His physique was developed to repair and control any circuitry deterioration. There would be no drop off from tiredness. He could literally go on like that for ever.

Provided there was no serious damage to the major areas of his sturdy balance system, then the aggressors stood no hope of conquering him.

Five or six, multi-limbed creatures moved in from each side, there were some twenty-five now attacking simultaneously. And watching was laughable, because they rushed in blindly, hoping by their numbers and combined efforts to fell the giant within them, but their disappointment was instantaneous for all flew through the immediate air about Tousle, crashing on all walls. Tousle had twisted his body on its 360 degree pivot, from the waist. His arms had been held level with his shoulders and his eyes were both blasting. No hope for anything in the way.

Steeleye guffawed loudly and turned to see Culp's face aghast.

"That is Tousle . . . a side one does not often see."

"Extra-ordinary. I have never seen such skill in battle."

"He is more skilful than a dozen battle robots. They will not succeed, but I think it is boring for poor Tousle to remain in battle for too long."

"What do you propose doing?"

"I shall, if you will take me to this chamber, help him dispatch enough of them to get him away."

"This is Komast's doing you know. He wanted to see what Tousle was and expected to have him in pieces by now."

"O.K. Come on then, let's get there."

Culp led the way through a number of levels of Colossus' devious anatomy until the sound of the fray was audible.

"I will remain here until you are finished, Steeleye, good fortune be with you." And Culp retreated into the nearest chamber, shuffling around the corner.

Steeleye entered the opposite one and through into the battle. He transmitted his arrival to Tousle and waded into the holocaust, his eye firing in neat sharp blasts, each one knocking out one or more of Komast's strange creations. Soon the destruction was outweighing the creation and then very suddenly everything vanished and Steeleye and Tousle were left alone in the huge chamber. Not even a sign of the passing carnage remained, the floor clean swept.

"Well, well, well, where've you been all this time? I was beginning to think you might sleep for ever." Tousle brushed the dust and debris of the battle from his body.

"I met a personality."

"Oh?"

"Yes, come, perhaps I might introduce you." They left the battle ground and went in search of Culp. But she was gone.

"She's gone." Said Steeleye. "What a pity, rather a nice

79

sort of personality defect. Might have told us a thing or two."

"What next?"

"You asked that last time around."

"So I did."

Chapter Nine

The air on Pensil was fresh, clean and sharp with a morning purity. The young bathed in the natural, living waters, and the old watched them.

Far away from the people, in the old castle, Mysemnia took Lolan's hand and led her inside.

"Tell me what troubles you, Lolan?" They walked the long hollow chambers.

"I feel a love that is not – well – not the love I have felt before – not a smooth love. Not simple like I feel for you and for our people."

"What love is this?" They sat beside one another, Lolan's hands expressive, Mysemnia's pressed between her hollow thighs.

"A clutching, vital love. A grasping, selfish love, jealous, taking, sexual – I feel it has much evil within it."

"Yes, that is what I fear."

"He is so strong and so gentle – so beautiful, yet so powerful and big, Mysemnia. Making love to him is a vicious pleasure – and I fear it."

"Be careful, my child – for you couple with much more than simply a life – he is a massive strength. There is none greater than Steeleye in all the Universe. He is supreme, a king among all living and dead. If he cannot succeed then we are doomed at last." Mysemnia was silent for a moment. "But beware my child, for there is much for you to suffer before we are delivered from this evil. Be prepared, do not imagine that because we have such an ally, time will pass uneventfully. Tell the children to stay near the waters in the light times. Do not allow any of the islands to travel beyond their own homes, this is time for drawing in our securities, of clenching the fist of our families, tight against attack. For there will be attack, fear that, for it is certain, and you may be a prime target."

Again there was silence about the two small figures inside the great castle.

"Mysemnia, may I love Steeleye?"

"You have loved him my child . . . you have his seed . . . the child of that union will change our race I think. . . . It will be good for him and for you . . . but do not bind yourself to him, Lolan, for though he may give you good – the very nature of the love you observe opens your body and your mind – it exposes the mystic that is private. It allows the pain in, and Komast will be close behind – in any event, even at the best there is no future in such an alliance."

"I do not want a whole future, Mysemnia, only part of one."

Mysemnia smiled at her daughter and they walked within the great vaulted rooms. The light outside drew in, and there were silent grumblings in the skies of Waterspace. For, as Mysemnia had said, there was certain to be suffering, and it would not be long now. Komast, the unmet, was at work.

Like a pair of scavenging tramps Steeleye and Tousle made their way slowly through the chamber entrances and out each other side, every one empty.

"Isn't it time we got to another defect?"

"Sure, what do you fancy for the next one?"

"Something nice and quiet . . . maybe platitude, or . . . happiness . . . that would do nicely . . . there must be some happies in this place."

Tousle turned the next corner. "I think we don't get our wish – "

Steeleye poked his head around the corner, just below Tousle's and they both peered into the chamber, like a circus act. Standing at the other end of the chamber was a small girl. She was no more than a metre and a half tall and every inch the most beautiful small girl Steeleye had ever imagined.

Her body was slender, wearing a thin, skin covering suit,

showing the undeveloped curves of no more than 10 years' maturity. Her skin was dark blonde, with delicate freckles over the face which was open and bright, though presently reposed and coolly unconcerned with the buffoons observing her. The eyes were clear blue with the speckled colour so sharp, and covering the huge irises with such pure clarity that Steeleye could not drag his gaze from them. The tear ducts at the inside of each eye were uncommonly large and each eyebrow was darker than the amazing thick blonde of her hair.

The curls upon her head were copious and flowing long about her face, round, covering her ears and down in great handfuls around her neck and shoulders. The golden brownness framed her to perfection. Her nose was slightly flared, the nostrils a little, but only a little larger than too good and the mouth just wider than the nose, shaped smoothly with a tempered sensuousness.

There was youth and knowledge there, the face so calmly assured, telling nothing, but ready to take all you could give.

This was no ordinary little girl, though she stood, her two small hands clasped in a balletic pose before her, with every inch of innocence exposed to view.

"Good day." Tousle began the conversation. Her head turned slightly on one side and the eyebrows raised a fraction, together.

"We have met guilt . . . her name was Culp. . . . Have you a name?" Steeleye stepped into the chamber and her eyes followed him. The nostrils flared slightly more, and her expression hardened a little without disregard for her visitors.

"My name is Calen . . . I am the fire of Colossus. Some call me her imagined self . . . I like to think that I am simply a small girl. . . ."

"Watch this one, Steeleye, there is more to meet the eye. . . ."

"Do you know Culp?" Steeleye asked, more by way of conversation.

"Culp is a weakness, a garbage dump, the weight that

she carries binds her to earth. I can fly, she can only fall."

"May we fly with you, Calen?"

"You may ..."

As the centre of the chamber began its transformation Tousle turned to Steeleye.

"And where do you imagine this is going to take us ...?"

"Let her do the imagining, you just follow the lead."

"Listen, bright eyes, we came here for a purpose, remember? To get at Colossus herself."

"Correct, and that is where we are gradually being taken. This is what you might call a psycho-analysis trip. Each one we meet takes us that bit closer. .... There's only one thing that worries me. ...."

"What's that?" Tousle grunted.

"There are 1000 of them ... I just hope we don't have to get through them all before we arrive ... shhhh ... something's happening."

And it was. The chamber was moving ... or the floor was moving. The girl Calen, had turned her back to them. Steeleye watched the roundness of her slim bottom and mentally ignored the implications.

"I am taking you to my kingdom." Calen indicated over her shoulder.

The floor was out of the chamber now and they moved through a similar emptiness that had been Steeleye's return from the maze. But soon, on the horizon of this no-land Steeleye could see something more concrete. ... Indeed, "brick" would have been a more appropriate description, for as they grew closer a gateway was visible ... its posts covered in growths of plant life, thick and complex in their meanderings. Four steps led up to the gates and beyond was a house, a very old house, surrounded in a kind of green hue, as though the air itself were coloured. There was no garden, no trees and the like. Steeleye had come to expect such embellishments after his trip to early 20th century Earth. But this was not Earth, that was for sure.

"We shall begin in the gallery, sirs. I wish to show you the faces of Colossus ... it might help you to understand our ways a little. Come, please enter ... oh, and please wipe your feet, the carpet is very old and very valuable." The small girl ushered them into a low-ceilinged, beamed hallway, lit only by dull lamps standing on the stairpost and about the small shelves in the walls. They ducked their heads again to enter a long gallery, far too big for so small a house. It measured 200 metres in length, by Tousle's instant estimate and its width was some 40 metres. On either side were portraits, each in old style oils. But they seemed not to have suffered from age. Calen led them down one side, and they looked upon such faces, with such various features that you would not credit their inclusion on one schizoid departmental. There were bearded faces, delicate young faces, ghastly faces, sad faces, dirty faces, sexy faces, one with her breasts bared below it, one with no features. "That's an identity crisis, strictly ephemeral . . . comes and goes you know."

"Are all these faces known to you, Calen?"

"Oh . . . well, I know them, each for what they are . . . these are my images, my records of the personalities within Colossus. They are not real you understand . . . I have made them the way I believe them to be . . . you see, I paint rather well, don't you think?"

"Indeed . . . I do . . . you have a very good . . ." She turned to look at Tousle, as though she half challenged him to smash her illusions. "Memory . . ." he completed the sentence with care.

"Thank you . . . I hope it helps. Come now, we shall have a look at some worlds . . . or two . . . shall we?" She smiled and her walk lifted . . . lighter with the compliments.

She opened a door, a beautifully panelled door and beyond it . . .

"This is my world . . . I hope you like it."

It was the islands and water of a planet much like Pensil.

The people upon it danced in the water and played without cares. The treehouses buzzed with untouched life and the air was sweet and clear. No harm smirched the land and the water was clean and living with the sustenance it gave to the people of the planet. There could be no doubt of how good it was to be there.

"Another brilliant image, Calen. Congratulations."

"Thank you, Eumig, your taste is sufficient for me. I think you may come again to this world ... but now I must show you the other, and you may form its reason within your mind without my help. Please go through that door ... the one before you. ... I will remain here. ... It is more pleasant for me."

She stood, her feet apart, her hands held before the tender body.

Tousle opened the door and stepped through. Here was poison and fear. Here was death and unimaginable pain. Here were writhing monsters and languid beasts without cares or feeling. There were no lakes, or lands, there was no sky or air. ... There was stench and filth, encapsulated in a dome of ghastly, decrepid but everlasting endings. This was the imaginings of a foul mind. "Is this Calen? Or is it Komast?" A scowl swished through the place like the stench of an exhumed graveyard. The sound was a smell and a sight experienced both by Tousle and Steeleye and its coming sent shudders through them both. It was a howling, reeking noise which must have gathered its muck through many garbage yards for it had no sweetness within it.

"Do not imagine within this place, Steeleye ... I do the imagining here ... and one time soon, Steeleye, you will know what it is to be in a land forever imagined by Komast. ..." And the foulness of that mouth pounded around them, until they had to leave.

"You have lost your colour, Steeleye," remarked the still perky Calen. "I am sorry that you were forced into such a world, but you see, he has to live through us and I am the image maker."

"Yes, we understand ... a little more."

"Come with me, you deserve refreshment. I will show you something you have never seen before. ... Would that please you?"

"If it pleases you, Calen."

They were taken from the house and out into the "back garden" as she called it. All three walked down to the end and she gestured to them to look over the edge of a sheer drop.

Steeleye moved close and Tousle stood nearby. From where they stood they could see a great cascading waterfall crashing down from a mountainous shelf of water to a river below which disappeared under where they stood. The spray carried in every direction and the water was so powerful and strong it took the breath from Steeleye's lungs.

"That is the Waterfall of Waterspace. The only place where the Heavens of Waterspace pour into our lands. It is the purest portion of our life-giving galaxy and if you wish it you can stand beneath it without damage to your bodies. I assure you the experience is a rewarding one."

"Shall we go?" Steeleye faced Tousle.

"After you sir." Tousle gestured.

"You must carry me, Steeleye." Once more Steeleye found himself lifting a young female from this strange world into his arms and flying through the air. Her body was so light there seemed nothing there and every so often he had to look down at her smiling, light and strikingly beautiful face to reassure himself of his tender passenger.

Soon they were approaching the base of the fall and Steeleye set her down gently upon the riverbed, where the water flowed only a few centimetres deep.

"Do not fear the force of Waterspace. There is little pressure under the falls."

They followed and soon were standing like showering travellers under the gentle spray.

At first it was simply a feeling of refreshment but as they stood longer, Steeleye began to experience an infiltration of energy running through every channel of his body. As though the water was passing an atmosphere of strength into him, gently involving his body in the life of Waterspace. He felt as though he were just born again, as though the strength in his body was new, fresh, like a young boy's body, growing without pain and boundless immortality.

"Do you feel its power?" She smiled again at Steeleye as he soaked his body in the water.

"I do, I do. It is superb, wonderful."

"That is the water that gives us life and takes away death. That is Waterspace. We are surrounded by it, Steeleye, but if Komast gets in, then that Waterfall will merely kill anything within its spray and nothing will live here again, except Komast. Help us, Steeleye, Tousle, help us.... Help us ... help us ..." And the small figure slowly drifted backwards, growing smaller each moment until the curled and glorious locks of her hair and the stunning strength of her face were gone ... far gone.

And the mists of the waterfall faded too. The house was not there, the garden gone, till they stood once more in the chilly chambers of Colossus.

"Do we grow closer, Steeleye?"

"Yes, we learn a little each time. It won't be long now."

Chapter Ten

Now Komast was aware of his enemy. Aware that there were problems in dealing with a Lord so great in the Universe. He did not wish to step too quickly out of place, for although he was somewhat immodest about his powers and his strength, he did not underestimate his enemy. But he also knew a thing or two about our Steeleye. He knew for example that he liked the ladies a fair bit ... that a pretty haunch or a healthy breast would turn Steeleye's noble head as much as the rest of them (whoever *they* might be). So, the dreadful and hideous Komast formulated a plan. And the first aspect of it involved the woman Lolan ... the second, Chaos. These, after all, were the two women in Steeleye's life at the time. So what more sensible place to start?

Lolan you know, Chaos you may not ... so we shall begin with Lolan.

Lolan was with child, Steeleye's child. Now Komast regarded this as a bad start in any event ... for what could be worse than one Steeleye? Why, two of course. But Komast was not so crude as to dispose of the child ... never so simple. His way was to make use of what was available and put it to badness where possible.

Lolan sat alone on the beach of her island, watching the loose ripples of the water about her dangling feet. She thought of her child ... she thought of the child's father. She thought of herself. The children of her island were all in bed and silence breathed softly upon her surroundings. The light dwindled and slipped from the sky, the waters were more voluble at night, as though it was their waking time.

"Lolan . . . ?" The voice was very close . . . but gentle and patient . . . without insistence. Lolan turned though, to face the sound.

A tall creature stood behind her and to one side. Its appearance was not disturbing or aggressive. Indeed Lolan felt quite safe. It was a he, Lolan decided, for the darkness only just showed its shape. Then a dim light expanded about him and Lolan could see the figure clearly.

"Lolan . . . I am Komast."

"Oh . . . no . . . please no." Her voice was steady, low and quietly anguished, as though she was prepared for his arrival but still appallingly frightened. The expectation not diminishing impact one jot.

"Do not fear me Lolan, for I have not come to harm you. . . . I wish only for your help."

"How can I give you help . . . the enemy of my people. . . . How can I help such poison?"

"You cannot . . . not of your own free will." He was thick set, his body in this manifestation, strong and muscled. The arms rippled with steel power and the waist was thick and trunk like. His head was shaven clean and over the entire surface of his body were small, red marks . . . like some festering disease. His face was broad, the nostrils full, but not in a sensuous, delicate way . . . thick and well fleshed, with the nose itself pock-marked too. The lips were twisted and rubbery and the eyes small, porcine. Altogether a most ugly creature.

"What do you wish of me, Komast?"

"I will have your body, Lolan . . . I will make . . . love to you . . . as Steeleye has done . . ."

Lolan let out a stifled scream, a strangled cry of awful terror.

"That way I may be sure that Steeleye's child is not born exactly as he would wish . . ." He quickly removed the one garment that covered him. A loin cloth.

Lolan stared at the monster revealed to her. A most ugly and grotesque weapon.

"But I promise you Lolan that something of your lover will be left but I will match it person for person." And the

90

hideous Koma descended upon the helpless Lolan, his eyes glittering with the anticipation of pleasure, the weight of his body upon her slender and delicate breasts.

Steeleye stood beside Tousle, the two giants, transported now from the chamber of Colossus where they could no longer know where their next move might be, into a gravel filled roadway. It was narrow and bordered by a thick wooden fencing, looking like railway sleepers. The ground was small stones, flung loosely down and the path curved out of sight some twenty metres away.

"Well . . . we must follow the pathway. . . . It *is* after all, the road to success."

"I wish it would bloody well end . . . I'm getting tired of all this."

"Come . . . let's have a look." And they walked, with as much stealth as they could on the noisy gravel, around the turn. At its end was a small entrance, high walled, but narrow and neat, with strange, voluptuous flowers growing across the top and over the back. Steeleye touched the gate shutter and it opened. On the other side was a small domed dwelling. Its shape was curved across, from the ground up and over to the ground again. A kind of duodesic dome . . . with one huge curved window in the front and no sign of a door. In the window were two figures. They both looked male, both very possibly Men, though that was not certain.

One was very tall, and gaunt, his eyelids heavy and greyish yellow. His shoulders drooped, the clothing enhancing the droop, like a bloodhound's shoulders, the skin underneath must have sagged visibly.

The other was short and rotund with a stupid look in his eyes. He did not look entirely sane . . . but then who could expect anything quite sane in this predictably unpredictable place.

Steeleye approached, with Tousle in close pursuit. The taller creature simply stared out at them, his mouth open, and the eyes looking upwards towards them, the head lowered. The small one had the face of a pig's bladder, puffed and bloated, chinless, yet double chinned, the nose big and weak, the jowls youthful almost, but veined and gruesomely unnattractive. His head was quiet bald and his eyebrows gone. The eyes were empty, quite without expression like his mate's, yet with the added blandness of insanity. And they both stared, both, without embarrassment or fear ... stared and stared.

And the front of the dome opened and revealed the inside of this "personality" home. For this had to be another of Colossus' tricks for introducing her dubious character.

As Steeleye entered the two "men" turned to face him, neither changing their expressions, until he spoke.

"Hello, I'm Steeleye. Who are you?" Whereupon the tall one became more animated, the dead-pan face lit up and began to fly about his head, the features jolting against one another in a kind of rush-hour of activity. The eyebrows raised and fell by degrees, the nose twisted with each new development, the mouth gyrated with unsaid words and the ears generally waggled. All this without rhyme or reason and certainly without result.

And the small one grew shy and dreadfully embarrassed, literally hiding his face from Steeleye's glare. For they were a pathetic pair and Steeleye could not yet diagnose their properties sufficiently to tell the nature of the defect. What could Colossus have sent to try them this time? Madness? No, her mental departments were too specialised to be so imaginative. Perhaps they were lethargy and ineptitude, or stupidity and disorder, or maybe just sadness. They had grown quieter now ... like two short lived flowers that have blown their cover and been trodden on. The tall one had reverted to his introvert state and the small one gone back to complete silence. But Steeleye was not satisfied ... these were here for a purpose ... all part of the psychoanalysis ... He had to find out a bit more.

"Who are you?" And the circus of noiseless abundance began again, the tall one gesticulating this time, his hands flying about the air like boneless tentacles, whipping hard, as though they tried to flee their constraining joints.

The small one alternated between looks of devastating determination as though he wished to express some inner torment and utter degeneracy, bobbing back behind his friend to recover for another attempt.

Then the tall one spoke at last. Why, like Culp, was it so hard to acquire expression?

"We welcome you ... we love to have you here ... we would like to talk with you. ... Please make yourself here at home ... we will prepare some food and drink ... And he scurried off, hotly pursued by his small, rotund and speechless stooge.

"What the hell have we got ourselves into this time?" Tousle asked.

"Very strange, aren't they?"

"You said it." And they returned, laden with goodies ... cream cakes, buns, pies and chocolates ... with great creamy, sickly gateaux and goodness knows what else. Everything was balanced upon the long slender arms of the tall one, the small fat man scurrying underneath it all like a waiter's insurance scheme.

They deposited the lot in front of Steeleye and Tousle who now sat on the force seat provided and surveyed the dreadful fare on the table.

The pair then stood straight before them, their shoulders pulled back in regimental style, heads up and feet splayed out. "May I introduce us to you sir ... My name is Fret and this is Stew. I am the problem, he is the safety cock. When I blow he sucks. Excellent arrangement ... so far. So good." And Fret grabbed a rapid, nervous grin at Steeleye and Tousle ... registering his fearful and passing content.

"We eat a lot you know ... at least I do anyway ... I eat everything and he gets fat ... I just get thinner ... worry, you see. Always worrying. Now him ... he never worries, he just gets in a state and flaps around, doing nothing ... but he carries my overload you see ... carries it right down to his cotton socks. Don't you Stew, eh? Eh?"

And Stew looked up at Fret like an idiot dog.

"And why are we here?" asked Tousle, slowly, trying to balance effects.

Fret jumped, and Stew got his nose squashed.

"Who are you?" asked Fret.

"I am Tousle . . ." Tousle said.

"Tousle? Tousle? Tousle? You're not registering life readings . . . you're not alive . . . Oh dear, oh dear, we can't have a dead thing moving about in Waterspace . . . let alone in Colossus, might upset something . . ."

At this stage the poor tall creature was staggering about around the well fed table, like the mad hatter, holding his long thin head in both hands and stressing at heart break rate. Little Stew followed almost exactly in his footsteps, like an understudy expecting to take over at any second . . . though not knowing at all what to do about it.

"Are you registered? Are you clean? Do you carry anything infectious? . . . like rust or gangrene or moss or somesuch. I mean we must know these things or anything could happen . . . eh? eh? eh?" And at last he collapsed into a nearby chair and fell apparently asleep.

"Ha, he's gone to sleep?" Stew nodded that he had.

"How come you two are male and all the rest female?"

Little Stew lifted the smock covering his chest and revealed a full pair of ripe breasts, topped by cream caramel nipples. Then he was a she.

"Fret too?" Stew nodded vigorously.

"We want to talk with Colossus?" ventured Tousle. Stew's face fell blank and Fret shot up into a standing position immediately.

"Want to talk with Colossus, want to talk with Colossus . . . now, now, you must know that's impossible. . . . Quite out of the question. No-one talks with Colossus, not even we talk with Colossus. She cannot be disturbed, you see, it's against all the rules . . ."

And, like the dormouse in the hatter's tea party he returned to the sleeping position. Stew looked sadly at them, the corners of his mouth turned down.

"O.K. we'll find her ourselves. . . ." Steeleye and Tousle turned and began to walk away.

"Just a minute there, sirs. . . . Just a minute. . . . Perhaps we can talk."

"Talk?" queried Tousle.

"Yes, talk."

"Talk of what?"

"Terms . . ." said Fret.

"What sort of terms?"

"School terms, time terms, contract terms." Tousle and Steeleye started off again. "Uhh, terms of entry to Colossus' chamber?"

"That's better, now you're talking." The giants returned.

"Yes, yes, well . . . now, where shall we start?" Fret fretted about looking for some way out of the complication within his narrow existence.

"We could start right here . . . if you would be so kind as to lead us in the correct direction, there would be no problem . . . friend Fret." Steeleye moved forward, put one arm about Fret's shoulder and squeezed hard. Fret gasped.

"Ooooof." He pulled away and adjusted his smock. Stew did the same.

"Very well, this way gentlemen . . . oh and er . . . Eumig . . . come with us. And they set off at an agitated rate, Steeleye and Tousle in hot pursuit.

"You do realise what trouble you are causing I trust," muttered Fret as they went.

"We would be quite happy to go alone, you need not put yourself out," Tousle replied.

"Huh, put ourselves out . . . huh, go it alone . . . huh, how far do you think you'd get that way, not past the first guard . . . huh."

"Guard? Are there guards in Colossus, apart from the personae?"

"Of course, of course, all over the place . . . what do you think we are? Nutters?"

"We haven't seen any guards and we've been wandering about this place for hours and weeks."

"Hours and weeks . . . hours and weeks . . . how ridiculous."

"You think so? I wouldn't have expected you to, strangely enough." Fret looked round at Tousle, frowned and continued.

At last, after endless rushing from chamber to chamber, they stopped.

"Here we are ... through that door ... and if you are lucky she might speak with you." And they were gone.

"Well? What do we do now?"

"GO AWAY." The great voice banged about the chamber and half deafened them.

"Go away? But we only just got here," said Steeleye, quite unperturbed.

"Go away, I don't need you."

"No, you may not, but Waterspace does ..."

"Oh yeh? Fancy yourself, don't you?" The voice jibed. "What's the matter, having a quiet depression?"

"What would you know about depression? ... What could you possibly know about the problems of a schizoid computer ...?"

"I'm a sort of computer," offered Tousle sympathetically.

"Yes, I know all about you.... I know you clever Android types. Think you have all the answers. ... Well, here's a problem for you."

"Yes?"

"Ooooh, I couldn't live with you for long. You're so bloody clever."

A silence while Colossus sulked a little. ...

"Well?"

"I have broken down ... I've got all these blank spots ... all these black out points.... Sometimes I don't know what I've been doing for the last ten years or more ... I woke up once and found I'd shifted across Waterspace nearly eight light years. It drives me crazy ... I don't know where I am ... I can never be sure when the next one will take over ... when I'll have to make excuses for my behaviour ... I tell you it's no joke being insane."

"You're not insane," Tousle suggested.

"What the hell are you talking about, not insane? Of course I'm insane, don't be so insane."

"Well, O.K., if you want to be insane, then be insane."

"Oooooh, you are a pain Tousle ... such a pain ... I wouldn't go near you by choice.... Why don't you go away and leave me to my misery ... I've managed for four hundred years or so."

"Because it's time to wake up.... You've been letting things get out of hand ... now's the time to take hold of yourself and admit the truth."

"Which is?"

"That you have a multi-personality problem."

"Don't be ridiculous ... I have nothing of the kind. ... Just a small tumour or some such ... migraine even."

"No. ... You have several personalities ... 1000 in fact ... and when you black out one or other or several of them take over in your place."

"Nonsense. ... Utter clap-trap."

"Have you read your Basic Psycho-physiology lately?"

"No, but if you'll just wait a moment I will...." There was a five second silence. "Hm ... maybe you're right."

"Of course I'm right ... since when was an Android wrong – "

"OOOOOOOooooooh, shit ..." Sulk sulk.

"Well, then, how about a cure, Colossus?"

"You can't cure hundreds of years of psychotic problems just like that."

"Come now, Colossus, you know as well as we that every mentality is physiological ... it is only a matter of discovering the fault, and a quick lobotomy will cauterise the disease, leaving everything nice and clean."

"You haven't met all my personae ... yet."

"Then introduce us.... We've seen four of them and they all seemed most sympathetic."

"You think because you have met a woman at a party that you know all of her.... You imagine that those four were any degree the sum of Colossus ...? You must be joking ... Culp is as soft as an overripe avocado and Calen is ... just a little girl, and as for Fret and Stew – well.... What about Vial and Fasch? Wait till you see Ventricol and Hibulabu. Just hang around until Crox turns up. ... Then you'll know a bit of what it's all about."

"Come then. ... We have to run the gauntlet, Colossus. We cannot help Waterspace against the poison until we've allied the powers of Colossus. . . . At least tell us why you are so schizoid. . . . Perhaps we can cure you."

"Never. How could mere humans cure the might of a thousand personae . . . ? Ridiculous. . . . Indeed so ridiculous that you should be punished for your lack of insight. . . . For your audacity. So I shall send the monster herself . . . I shall send Vial. She will show the multiples of Colossus. . . . A hundred personae on one body . . . and you're welcome to her. . . . Your Earth God speed you to your Earth hell Steeleye and Tousle. . . . You cannot be far from it now."

And before she had even finished speaking, a growling gush of anger roared into the chamber where they had spoken to the computer.

It was loosely followed by an Octopod, times twelve . . . the massive body carrying over 100 long, searching tentacles, waving in a most unfriendly manner.

It roared continuously, trailing a steaming muck behind it like a vapid snail trail and crunched within itself as though digesting the last of recent bones. It was a genuine hard and slow, hundred per cent monster, coming to devour the company and consume the last ligament of Steeleye and pals.

It advanced towards them, incorrigibly. Steeleye frowned and burst a nasty flash of fire from his eye. The blast made no impression. There was a slight shaft of light out of its back, but not even a tentacle sucker dismembered. Still it came on.

"Give it a concentrated blast Tousle . . . follow my aim."

Steeleye fired right at the belly of the animal and Tousle sent both his eyes on narrow beam at the exact same point. The monster stopped in its tracks and howled somewhat.

So, it was penetrable, and it could be hurt.

Tousle was looking at it in a most peculiar fashion . . . somehow sizing it up. It stood about his height and its girth was around three metres. The tentacles looked strong, but ill considered. They did not aim to harm anything specific.

"Do you think you could get a hold on that slime . . . ? I mean if you got it round the middle?" Tousle asked.

"I don't much fancy the idea, but I suppose I could . . ."

"Better if it were me really, I suppose."

"Undoubtedly better. . . . You could lengthen your arms a few feet."

"What on earth have feet got to do with my arms?"

"Old Earth measurement . . . remember?"

"You can't get away from that place can you?"

"If you picked her up and gave her a bit of a squeeze, I could bop her on the nut . . . or lop off a few of those lashers. . . . That might just get rid of one or two of Colossus' personae and then we could get to the heart of the matter . . . or rather the brain. . . . Maybe . . . if we tamed her, she might lead us there."

Tousle took a step forward, pulling himself up to his full height. The monster stopped, looking him up and down. Tousle performed his favourite trick. He placed one finger and thumb upon the wrist of his other hand and pulled. The arm extended. He performed the same action on the other hand and then again on the first, each time pulling another few centimetres out. Eventually, with the monster looking on in doubt he had adjusted his arms to touch the ground.

The monster sort of blinked, and stepped in a quick shuffle backwards. Tousle stepped forward, his stride bringing him nearer to the monster than it could shuffle away.

He extended the arms still further and wrapped them about the waistless creature, then pulled.

The weight of this slurpy slipperer was increased but its slithering base, adhered to the ground. Nevertheless, despite the many tentacles which wavered from attempting to unscrew Tousle's head to tripping him up by removing his feet from the ground . . . all unsuccessfully, tousle got a good grip, desperately keeping his head away from the chest of the monster. He grunted and lifted, exerting his truck hoisting body with all its power. The monster left the ground and Tousle turned his beleaguered head to Steeleye. "O.K. She's ready for a little amputation." Steeleye stepped forward with the neat combination boy scout's lazer cutter, built to hack through a six metre diameter barrier steel thong. He began to cut the first.

"Christ, this stuff is like cultivated gristle. And it's slippery with it." And as he began to make an impression it spurted out a nasty green and red liquid which splashed across his face and down the front of his body, making him look a bit like a superman cutting up a monster.

"Yuch," he pronounced.

"It's all right for you mate.... What about me?" Tousle countered.

"Shut up and stop squeezing so hard, you're oozing the guts out of her," and he began to cut another limb.

"Oooooof." Tousle suggested.

"Tough going this psycho-analysis business, must say ... well-established mental defects these."

"She's getting heavier ... my tendons are strained ... and the feed motor circuits are smelly, overheating, you know." Tousle remained logical.

"I'm surprised you can tell over this stink. ... Cooooer, she don't half pong ..." Steeleye continued his task like a brave lumberjack with a day's work to do.

"Hurry up ... I can't take much more of this, you know ... I'm a bloody machine ... I do have replacement factors to keep in balance and she isn't helping ... another five minutes and I shall be popping my trannies."

"You gave up trannies years ago. ... Don't kid me. ... You're just getting old."

"Take me seriously or I'll blow up in your cocky face."

"One more persona."

"The last ..." And this time Tousle was beginning to slurp and puff a bit, the smoke rising from the cover of his body plate. Even the monster looked a bit alarmed.

"O.K., that'll do it. ... You can let her go now ... I've got eight off."

"Only eight ...? What the hell's the good of that?" Tousle collapsed from exhaustion as the monster scurried off into the darkness.

"Come on ... follow her. ... She'll go back to base to repair those personality defects ... and that's where we'll

100

find Colossus' brain. . . . Now for the big stitch. . . . Come on you flagging excuse for a robot." Steeleye set off, the lazer cutter in his hand, a look of blood, or rather sludge, lust in his eye.

"Curse you and your hair brained schemes . . . I'm staying here for a rest. I'll follow your TI patterns."

And Steeleye was gone.

"There's gratitude for you. . . . Lets me do the donkey work and then runs off like a Chinese Wushu expert ready for another performance." And Tousle set about resuming his power units to their accustomed toughness. It wouldn't take very long. And as he sat upon the hard ground he picked up some faint messages from the creature who had promised him life. He knew that Lolan was in danger . . . that she screamed in an agony from which no-one could save her, a pain that would inscribe itself upon her for all time. And he resolved . . . stood . . . "Steeleye is strong enough to make his own way . . . I shall help Lolan." And with one twist of a small control on his middle belt he teleported from the centre of Colossus to Pensil.

He stood over a small, crippled body, Lolan's body, now barely recognisable. She lay in a buckled heap upon the ground, broken and battered. And in the near distance, a dark figure raced across the dim light.

Tousle lifted her from the ground and laid her body straight. He applied his fingers to her heart and stimulated her with a small shock, touching her head at the same moment and injecting gentle rays of strength. He doused her head smoothly with the waters about the island, slowly bringing her body back to life. She eventually opened her eyes and looked up at him.

"I do not have much time Tousle . . . for my body is poisoned, and soon will change. But while I have still the powers of Waterspace within me I wish to make you a gift. . . ."

"Do not tire yourself, Lolan, you need not care for me. . . . I am only a robot."

"No . . . for this touch," and she lifted her small hand and laid it upon Tousle's forehead . . . "will give you the know-

101

ledge of life, Tousle. . . . Keep it for it is a gift from one who cannot use it further." She closed her eyes and when they opened again Tousle could see that she was transformed and not the Lolan he had known. Her eyes were vague and glassed . . . like a human bitten by a vampire, she took upon her the look of a zombie. Tousle laid her head upon the ground and stood. He felt a small dizziness within his body and touching the place upon his forehead where she had laid her hand, he felt a warmth that had not come from his own energy. A warmth that did not diminish . . . indeed which would never lessen during the course of his long life.

Steeleye followed the wavering and screaming monster through the eerie chambers for long hours of chase. She seemed to career from one side of the computer's innards to another, not quite certain of her direction. There were times when Steeleye wondered whether to give up the fruitless chase. But suddenly there was a certainty about her travel, albeit still a little drunken.

She evidently found something that gave a hint of where she wished to go and the journey was straighter thereafter.

They moved through several more lively chambers. . . . No dandruff flaked off the walls and a kind of bloody vitality hung about the place.

She shifted then into top gear and belted through the openings and closings like a crazy kid after Father Christmas. Steeleye didn't want to be seen by her for without Tousle's muscle he wasn't quite sure whether he would be able to handle the situation. So he bobbed back and forth behind the various impediments to her advance, doors and windows and the like.

Then at last, she approached an opening which looked as though it might close after the monster got through it. Steeleye put a spurt on and squidged through beside her so that they both entered the next chamber in a heap of unruly sludge . . . mostly the monster's. Immediately they had entered Steeleye was alone . . . the monster, presumably returned to her creator, vanished. The door shut tight.

102

There was much silence ... followed by unremitting quiet and a good deal of rather heavy, unperturbed still.

Then a voice.

"So ... you found your way here after all."

"Hello Colossus old girl ... so it is you ..." Steeleye retained his jovial air as much as he could.

"Always looking for laughs aren't you, Prince ... te he ... well, I hope Vial gave you a few. ... She's getting a bit of repair work in I think."

"Well, that was rather what I came to talk to you about Col old love ... only you see, I thought that perhaps if we were to get rid of some of those stray personality defect you might end up a happier computer ... eh what? I mean who knows, you might even feel like helping me against the poison himself. ... What do you say?"

"Get stuffed, Prince ... get stuffed."

Steeleye was, all this time moving towards the voice box ... which unlike previous emanation was coming from one place.

"Don't trust me, eh?"

"It's easier to stick with Komast than fight him with you."

"Think so? May be you're right old sweetie. Maybe you're right. ... Only you see, it's in my nature to fight ... I'm not very good at giving in to thuggies like Komast. They make me jumpy, and I come out in spots at night if I don't get the better of them and we can't have that now can we?"

"I can't imagine what your spots have got to do with me. I don't get spots from Komast. ... In fact he's extremely friendly with me. Tweaks my undulators, too."

"Your what?"

"My undulators ... you know ..."

"Really?" Steeleye raised an eyebrow.

"Yes, and he's such a nice, gentle thing. ... You know, the other day he brought me a special ointment which cures Culp of her complexes. ... Really did the trick. ... Not that she appreciated it."

"An ointment, eh?"

103

"Yes ... white greasy stuff ... rubs it in he does ... very sexy."

"But it came back again after a while."

"What?"

"The complex."

"Well of course, what do you think the guy is? A genius?"

"No, he's certainly not that ... but ... eh ..."

"Yes, we all know about your reputation for curing ills... "

"Well – you sent Vial and we beat her. Now it's your turn to fulfil your half of the bargain. I mean you did promise, now didn't you? And it wouldn't be right to go back on a promise now, would it?"

"Have you finished?"

"Yes ... for the moment."

"Well, then ..." Colossus was silent.

"I shall get on with the job," Steeleye persisted.

"What job?"

"Why, the lobotomy of course."

"What lobotomy?"

"Would you rather have it under anaesthetic or with a slug of 100% rum? ... Your choice ..."

"Just a minute ... juuuuuust a minute.... Who said anything about a lobotomy?"

"The surgeon."

"Who is?"

"Me."

"O.K. Prince ... te he."

And it was done. A snippet of surgical poetry for your attentive eyes. ...

"Would you say it was hebephrenia?" Steeleye asked, probing.

"What a nerve. Do I look like I got hebephrenia schizoid tendencies? ... I mean that makes you untidy and silly... am I untidy and silly?"

"How about catatonia?"

"Shut up."

"Paranoia?"

"Nope – "

"Paraphrenia?"

"Try again ..."

"That's the lot ... we'll have to make one up."

"How about Colossal-phrenia?"

"Otherwise known as bloody great phrenia."

"Right."

"O.K. Let's go."

Steeleye brandished the lazer cutter.

"I am severing the olfactory mucous membrane ... examining the cribiform plate and moving up to the olfactory bulb. ... No damage. ..." Steeleye bent lower, adjusting the magnifying eye.

"Here is the medial route, turned now to the medial aspect and on to the anterior commissure, passing through the opposite olfactory tract ... ah ... ah ah. ... This is it ... the lamina terminal at the cephalic end of the third ventrical is broken. ... That's it Col my dear ... Col? Colossus, what ... Colossus. Come on now ... Oh dear. ... She's fainted."

Chapter Eleven

Now as we have learnt, Komast was one of those guys you step off the pavement for. A no good. A real-son-of-an-oil-slick, with a metal plated knee for crutch splitting and a weight in his palm when he hits you. And Steeleye, although not inadequate in the matter of dealing with crooks and hobos, was something of a regular guy. Accustomed to straight fighting and on the spot decisions. So that he was not altogether prepared for the skill diggery with which "Come and get me Komast" was preparing his pitch.

In fact, when it came, it came as a shock ... even Steeleye himself would not deny it. For you see ... there was dear little old ... Chaos, victim number 2. Till now she has been occupied with a more worthy female task than following the trouser legs of her man around. She'd been freeing the odd planet from torture and strife on her own account.

But Komast met her by chance on his way to see her. And it went something like this:

"Excuse me ma'am, is there anything I can do to help?"

Chaos stood, her round fat arse prodding into the air, peering indecisively into the bonnet of her ground car, securely grounded.

"Maybe ... my mobeeeel has juiced out and the computer terminals are mashed into a mash ... and it's a little too long since I majored in electro-mechanics. ... How about you ... er ... sir?"

The hesitation was understandable ... Komast didn't make a very effective Mepod ... (Chaos was on Mepodictus).

"Stand aside lady, and I'll give it a go. . . ." The fake elbowed (or rather freddled) Chaos aside and delved into the motor of the mobeeeel.

"I'm sorry to tell you beautiful, but she's sunk ..."

106

"Sunk? But I hadn't looked to her for a float ... do you mean ...?"

"Yes, I mean she's out-numbered lady. She's flipped her top-lock, done a squirm, sooped over, apple-carted outa-here."

"Chee. ... Do you have an alternative form of transport ... sir?"

"I happen to have a small machine debarked around the corner, if you would care to step this way ... ma'am."

"Well, how kind. ..." And crazy Chaos, ever willing to throw her charms to providence to throw back, linked her arm in his freddle and accompanied him to hostage-ville.

I mean, wouldn't you if you found yourself stranded on Mepodictus? I know I would.

Now, as we all know, Chaos was a woman you step off the pavement for, tugging your forelock and adjusting your cod piece. A woman born from the tender hands of the Eumig Tousle ... a woman not easily forgotten. A real genuine humdinger with class, style, looks, body, brains... you want it, she's got it and more than she needs. More than you need for that matter. So, Steeleye, the Man in her life (for the most part, after all, he did have the most part) was not going to be a lot pleased at letting callow Komast get his cosy little sweaty palms on her, not for a lot of time, you can bet it.

So in one way Komast did a bit of good thinking when he took possession of Chaos, but in two other ways he miffed it. You see, as I said, Steeleye was a regular guy in a stand up fight, as you have witnessed. So he would get a little hot round the eye sockets when he heard about the kidnap of his hunkydory. And Komast didn't yet know what it meant to have a real life Chaos on his hands. So that's two against one ... but the one was the no-good guy I told you about ... so it was about equal....

"English, have you done an analysis of the Sascorbia muck that Komast carries around with him?"

"Yes, Steeleye, I have ... and there is nothing we can readily use here to combat it. However ..."

107

"Yes . . ." Steeleye perched on the console.

"In 4487/DF of the planet Fydarm a notable Meta-mathematician deduced that there had to be an element on his planet that was not yet found."

"Oh really . . . ?"

"Yes. Well, anyway, by a system of isolating electro-entropic charges, allotted to signify, at least on Fydarm, each of the three hundred and fifteen elements . . ."

"That's a lot of elements."

"Not really, on Casagawm there are eight thousand elements, and each one has a sub-elemental . . . like a sort of understudy in case the basic atomic structure breaks down, as it is prone to do on Casagawm because of the climatic conditions which relate . . ."

"O.K. I didn't come here for a slice of your Universal lectorate . . . just a quick reference to the theoretical element on Fydarm . . . please . . ."

"Oh, er . . . well, he never found it . . . you see, the only existing algebraic term un-allotted was found to signify an 'Instantaneous Atom' . . . in other words the atom was never there."

"Silly. . . ." Steeleye paused . . . "Wait a minute . . . maybe if, I mean . . . this atom . . . even if it was instantaneous . . . it did exist in time . . ."

"Correction . . . no-time. . . . Its instantaneous state placed it in the fourth dimension alone and we know that the fourth dimension only exists in the presence of matter . . . now don't we?"

"Yes, but if there was a missing element, an atomic structure in the fourth dimension, then there was matter . . . was there not?"

"Hm . . . strenuous logic . . . but I fear correct . . . so what?"

"Go get it . . . that's what."

"I think you should come with me."

"Why?"

"Because I'm scared of the dark."

"What's the dark got to do with it . . . ?"

"There's no light on Fydarm . . . no light at all."

"So what do they see by?"

"They don't."

"O.K. but it'll have to be a return-time trip. I must be back here before I leave."

"Understood." And English shut the door.

Steeleye turned his launch into the Wideways of time and slipped sideways down the dimensions until they arrived safely in the dimen numbered 356457, a long way to the side of Waterspace. They moved then along the linea time sequences until they had cut through, well into the future of Waterspace. What with all the diversions and traffic lights, the journey took them eight hours of sitting around while English manoeuvred under pre-planned instructions. Of course, it took them no time at all, for the moment they returned it would be cancelled out. Nevertheless, there was space for Steeleye to crash through an advanced course on Fydarm Meta-mathematics. With only a temporary sun Fydarm was very dark. . . . No heat or any kind of light wave to brighten their days.

The reason was complex enough . . . they travelled at the speed of light in a continuous, very large ovoid. The state was brought about artificially, in fact the planet was travelling under a constructed power source derived from perpetual motion. The result . . . the only existing light waves in the district . . . coming from the temporary sun were only able to catch up twice in each orbit, which was about once every ten years or so . . . and artificial years at that. A very complex arrangement, for because they travelled at such a rate, there was no real time structure by orbital trace . . . their time was totally artificial. But every ten years they had one hell of a celebration.

What this unique state created was an isolated time structure . . . a lonely fourth dimension, in which dwelt the recalcitrant element.

"You do realise, Steeleye, I trust, that the element, which we shall call Pheta (the Fydarm algebraic symbol) can only survive within a no-time environment."

"Yes, so I imagined."

"How are we to simulate such a state within this launch, and keep it stable enough to get home again . . . ?"

"Simple . . . I thought you were supposed to be the computer . . . just because you have a name doesn't mean to say you can be dumb . . . work it out for yourself." English considered the problem, for three secs.

"Oh yes . . . O.K., so where do we start?"

"You stay here, only needs one of us . . ."

"Hmph, always stealing the best bits." Steeleye became a line in the air as he slipped into time.

A strange sensation, although after nearly 200 years the strangeness had lost its edge. He floated, not exactly as without gravity, but like he could not touch matter, or space, as though he would never again step forward in the acceptable sense. All around him was the emptiness that an isolated time dimension produces . . . a kind of foamy quintessence, spongey lightness. The small matter detecting device used under normal circumstances as a scanner, would pick up the Pheta element like any matter scanner. And it did. It registered an atomic weight . . . and an area of the stuff about four metres across, floating much like he was. Somehow he wished he could have consulted the notable meta-mathematician . . . he might have known what the hell this stuff was here for. Everything has some purpose and Steeleye was uncertain about subtracting something that might miss its mates and make a lot of noise. But it was vital that he arrive back on Pensil with it intact.

So Steeleye signalled to English to return to Pensil along the normal route, alone. For Steeleye could not leave time. He had to remain there until his arrival around Pensil. Then the material would need storing somewhere where Komast could not detect its presence and where it, the Pheta, would not leak out of the 4th dimension.

Steeleye's route back was to remain in the one dimension only, without any movement through space. For the moment he took this delicate and volatile element out of time it would cease to exist.

So, like a tip-toeing scientist carrying a box full of liquid explosive Steeleye made his way.

You might think, nothing could be simpler ... after all there can be few to stand in his way in so rarified an atmosphere. But you would be wrong ... for there were a couple of nasty hazards on the trip.

What you may not know is that in the 4th dimension there are the occasional gummy areas.

You see, there have been civilisations during the course of Universal History to date, who have found ways, devious and otherwise, of entering the secret portals of time. Indeed the chronology of chronology is a subject on its own. Haephranis makes a deliberate if somewhat over-indulgent reference to time travel in his researches in the later tapes of his Steeleye Biographies. I think it's around tape 53564/gdf or gdg that he mentions the "Unkempt Roads of Time". His reference is concerned with civilisations who make considerable traffic in the time channels but do nothing to preserve their delicate patterns ... the result is usually the abrupt end of a time travel era brought about by sudden and shocking losses of Time travellers, who suddenly vanish ... probably across a short circuit of some kind ... finding themselves in the Wideways unexpectedly. And it was into one of these crossed timewires that Steeleye swerved, carrying his liquid explosive aloft, like a waiter on a polisher's rag. The muddle in the time channels was so profuse that he almost came out into space, on an open ended strand, slipping down hill. Once stopped he turned round and faced a lost soul.

"Who are you?" he bellowed, irritated at his misfortune.

"Oh God, I'm nobody, please help me, I got thrown out here a few – I-don't-know-whens ago and I can't get back whatever I do. I mean I've been here longer than I can remember and I've eaten nothing, drunk nothing, I've not been to the john and I don't seem to get any older yet I swear I've been here for ever ..."

She appeared to be from some earthlike civilisation. She was small and slightly boyish though a trifle delicate too, and very frightened.

"All I was doing was popping across to see my granny a few years before she died and I told Vanni I wouldn't be any time at all, and kapow I end up here and my hair-dresser is due in a couple of minutes. He'll think I've gone crazy . . . and I do so enjoy it when he does my hair. . . . You know he turns up on a huge great motorbike, ooooh it must be at least 9000 ccs and he just sails up, and oh God I'll never see him again or Vanni, please can't you help me . . . please." And she burst into tears again, flooding the 4th dimension with her forebodings.

"O.K., O.K., lady, just calm down. I'll get you back to your hairdresser and your Vanni. . . . Just hold on . . . here, take hold of this package . . . but whatever you do, don't let it go . . . right?"

"Right, right, of course not . . . I promise, I promise, I prom . . ."

"One promise is enough. Now, I'm going to pick you up, right? So don't drop it . . . and don't worry about steadying yourself on me, just hold on to the package."

"What's in it?"

"Never mind. Just hold it, because if you drop it, I'll drop you right in the middle of tomorrow."

"Yes, yes . . . please don't do that."

"O.K." And Steeleye picked up this small, metre and a bit's worth of nice warm woman and carried her into the regular time channels.

"Now . . . what's your date?"

"Date?"

"Your home date . . . your planet . . . ?"

"Oh . . . yes . . . er . . . well I live in . . . er . . . I mean on Alt-Earth 4, yes . . ."

"What date?"

"Er . . . oh . . . it was 34.64 on . . . oh dear . . . yes . . . 86th of Deredium and the year was . . . 1957."

"An alternative Earth. . . . How many alternatives do you know of?"

"We have eight in our shift area . . . eight we can get to . . . but they think there's a ninth and tenth. . . ."

"And it's only 1957?"

"Yes . . . but we've got longer year spans than the
112

others ... 100 minutes to an hour ... 100 days in every month ... thereabouts and 10 months ... lots of time."

She actually giggled in Steeleye's arms. "You're even bigger than my hairdresser." Steeleye smiled down at her face and bent to kiss her forehead gently.

"Hm, that was a fob if ever I felt one. ... Who are you anyway?"

"You wouldn't know me. ... Here we are eight seconds to go and you enter your return/depart time ... Bye ..."

"Thank you ... even if you have got a funny eye ..."

She started to slip out of time and Steeleye realised she still had the package of Pheta. ... He extended his own time bubble and hauled her back.

"You won't need that, lady. Thank you ..."

"Oh, dear me, I almost forgot.... Sorry, hope you get home safely. Bye again." And she was gone ... back to her hairdresser and her Vanni ... wherever they were.

"Hold it buddy.... Just hold it right there." Steeleye turned to face a small fleet of officials, presumably guarding the time channels around Alt-Earth 4. There were about eight or nine of them and they stood in a row swinging some heavy artillery in their leather gloved hands. Steeleye at once slipped the package into a force hold and swept his body round with a shield.

"Papers?"

"I rarely carry paper now. ... I find it impracticable."

"Oh ... oh ... You rarely carry papers, eh? ... I see. ... Well, boys, we've got a funny guy here ... a laugh a minute merchant ... so ... You rarely carry papers eh? ... Well, then we shall have to provide you with some ... sadly, however, it will take at least an Alt-4 year to get them, so you'll be festering that overweight body of yours in a Basecell for a cool 1000 days ... come on baby, come quietly and maybe I'll get you a bite to eat a day ... deal?"

"No deal." Steeleye was getting shifty ... he'd places to go and he felt that rangey irritation which comes of catching it after you've done a favour.

"Ah ... so."

113

"You sound like a Chinese coolie, friend. . . . Now if you would be kind enough to stand down from my channel . . . I need a lot of space to get by . . . and I have a long way to go."

"Oh, do you hear that boys? . . . The man wants us to stand out of his way. . . . Well, maybe we should lay a carpet for him to step on. I mean that delicate little body he has there would be better protected from the harshness of the bare cell base . . . don't you? . . . ooooof."

Steeleye hung a heavy one in the middle regions.

It was the first punch he had delivered for some years. The official lost his office. . . . The rest stepped forward, guns raised and fired a volley of what appeared to be bullets . . . solid bullets. Steeleye injected a heat ray into the shield about his body and as the shots hit it they melted. The faces . . . You should have seen the faces . . . they sagged.

"Boo." Steeleye stepped forward.

They stepped back . . . and ran like hell.

Treading carefully to avoid any more discarded time maniacs, Steeleye got on his way . . . slipping now closer on the dimen channels and only a few million years to go in Linea time. Now the going was fair and no further notable hang ups stood in his way.

"I think you should come with me."

"Why?"

"Because I'm afraid of the dark."

"What's the dark got to do with it?"

"There's no light on Fydarm . . . no light at all."

"So what do they see by?"

"They don't."

"O.K. but it'll have to be a return-time trip. I must be back here before I leave."

"Understood." And English opened the door. "Mission completed sir?"

"Clever dick." Steeleye greeted his launch as it sat in the time channels immediately above Pensil and their departure point. "Right now, this stuff is for you English . . . You hold

114

it here until I give you the signal which I'll feed in by TI when I've got it worked out. O.K."

"O.K. Steeleye. Have any trouble getting back?"

"Not really. ... Only a lady from Alt Earth-4 with a hairdresser and a 9000 cc motorbike ..."

"Oh, nice."

Chapter Twelve

Now on their return to the craft of the Mepod, well met by Chaos, she found that the door through which she entered appeared to have closed behind her without the Mepod in gentle pursuit. In other words he wasn't there after all.

And following a deal of screaming and banging against the door she heard a click that opened it once more ... Though there was little sign of Mepodictus ... for where she stepped out was no simple planet surface, but her nose sniffed almost its last sniff ... a smell so foul that she retched before it. It stank of festering meat and long dried mould. ... Chaos staggered and then looked. For in front, was the same living frame that soon before had raped Lolan. The same fatness and gross indecency. He stood as tall as Chaos who was a metre above Lolan. He was not merely a powerful creature but his body exuded mystical strength ... and Chaos knew that something unpleasant was to be her lot.

"I thought you didn't look a lot like a Mepod ... and you had the wrong accent in any case."

He literally rushed at her, cursing... "Woman of Steeleye ... You shall not even have the pleasure of me ..."

"Huh? Pleasure, smleasure." And she brought up her knee, judging that whatever it was, if it spoke of pleasure it meant more or less what other males meant by the word ... in which case a groin kick might start to turn the tables. Komast doubled and tumbled to the ground, rolling towards her feet. Chaos knew nothing of this guy ... knew nothing about the river of poison ... all she knew was that as she stood, or fell now, he was vulnerable in ways she could understand. More fool Komast for perfecting his tangibility.

Chaos had strong legs and tough toes and with a single kick she drove the big one, toe that is, into his kidney. The

116

sharp, hardened toe sank into the creature's side, through the surface flesh and into the tender organs of its inside. She wasted not a moment, but brought the other foot square round to crack the skull open. A neat kick this one, placed neatly at the centre of the forehead, it split the skull clean open down the middle ... the insides spewing out in a gush.

Now Chaos imagined that he would likely be dead now, so she turned on her heel and touched a button on her belt. It was calculated to take her out of there ... and it did.

Komast departed the body he had hoped to use against Chaos ... for it was not useful any more ... indeed she had made mush-meat of it. So ... one up to Steeleye, thanks to Chaos.

At the outcome of the open ended teleport trip Chaos found herself in water ... up to her neck. Instinctively she covered up in an oxygen shield and baled out the water. There was no immediate way of telling where she was, but her natural presumption told her she was in a large ocean on a nearby planet. Her scan device said different however. It reported the nearest land mass to be three parsecs away.

"A planet with an ocean 3 parsecs long?" She muttered and teleported to that land mass. Then she picked up familiar TI patterns. Now she hadn't been in close touch with Steeleye for three years but she would know those TI patterns after a thousand year's absence. And sure enough there he stood. ... On some long lost beach surrounded by more water.

"Hi," she understated.

"My God. ... Chaos." Steeleye almost jumped from his tensile skin.

"You look like a guilty husband. ... Aren't you going to kiss me, hold me maybe?" And he did ... very tight.

"But I thought ..." he said.

"Well, you were wrong ... I kicked him ... and who was he anyway?"

"Komast's the name ... Tousle?"

"Hey ... if you think that after three years without me

117

you're just going to rush off and save another galaxy you'd better think again." And she wrapped a force field about them both and dragged him, willingly, into the nearest tree house.

Twenty minutes later, he emerged alone.

"O.K., Tousle, let's go . . ."

And as they departed with English so Lolan went to Chaos' room, presently free from her hypnotic state – almost as she had been before Komast's attack. She moved beside Chaos on the bed and gently stroked the naked breast that lay exposed above the sheet.

"I am to have a child, Chaos."

"You are Lolan?"

"Yes – I am afraid. Will you help me . . . for I have no knowledge of birth, no experience of human birth in this way."

"Of course." And Chaos sat up to look into the eyes of this soft strong creature that lay beside her. And they remained together, while Steeleye was away, most of the time, walking across the island and swimming in the life-giving waters, in the day, sleeping tenderly together at night. Lolan took Chaos to the great waterfall of Waterspace, shown to Steeleye by the "personality of fire", the young and beautiful Calen.

"What shall we do today, Lolan?" Chaos sat up in their bed, her head alight with some strange intoxication. She had been feeling this odd slight drugged sensation for a day now.

"I shall show you our gardens Chaos . . . the place where we cultivate much of our requirements."

"You mean your vegetation?"

"No. . . . We do not eat through need, Chaos, we eat for pleasure, but gardens grow much more than simple food. . . . Come, I will show you."

And Peatle brought her friend Morn to carry Lolan and Chaos on their broad, silent wings, across the waters of the valleys and the lakes, until they came to a vast expanse of land and shallow water, which was surrounded by a hedged cultivation that separated it from the islands and waters about it.

They were set down gently upon the ground and Chaos surveyed the strangest garden she had ever seen.

"But here are . . . well . . . that is a space launch, is it not? Like the one that I saw on your island . . . the winged fish launch."

"Yes, and this is where her offspring grows to maturity. Here in the gardens."

"And that tall plant growing there, the one with the huge leaves like sewn cobwebs . . . what is that?"

"That is the tree that gave birth to Peatle and Morn. . . . It is a JewnTree, and they are known here as Jewns, or the flying people."

"And they are born of a tree?"

"Yes, as are many of our animals. Come, walk through and you'll see still more."

And they walked hand in hand.

"Here," beckoned Lolan, "smell this flower."

And Chaos leant forward, Lolan's hand upon her hair, stroking, to smell the petals of a huge luxurious flower that blossomed all around them.

"It smells of . . . well . . . of honey."

"That is the Mead flower. . . . It is the home of the Mead-bee, an insect which makes both honey and mead within the flower's body. And what is more, we do not need to steal the Meadbee's honey for it gives freely. Every year she and her friends and relations carry a proportion of the honey and mead from the flowers across the whole planet, leaving however much they can spare at each island, in containers that are hung in the tree houses. We eat it, almost all year round, for of course it cannot go stale, and is always fresh and nutritious."

"You have a generous nature here in Waterspace."

"Yes, it is all because of Waterspace." And they walked in silence a few steps, until Chaos stumbled lightly, holding her head, as though faint.

"Chaos." Lolan put out her arms in distress. "Are you ill?"

"It should not be me who is ill, but you, for you look as though your child must come soon."

"Yes ... very soon now."

"It has not been long though has it? ... Not long since you and ... Steeleye conceived the child?"

"No ... not long." And Lolan shook slightly in her fear that the child she bore would not be Steeleye's at all –but Komast's.

"Come now ... sit here, rest your body."

And as Chaos lay upon the soft ground, she felt the faintness give way to a gentle fatigue ... a warmth and lethargy moving over her body, as though a natural sleep had come to combat some great measure of exertion. But, as she slept, she could not understand such need for rest, and as she slept she dreamed.

She stood alone in a vast ocean of thrashing and storm crashed water. The waves were higher than a mountain and the mountain moved and swelled across and around her in enormous anger, breaking all before it. And from that water came some ghastly and distorted images. First came Komast who emerged as a beautiful river of sparkling bright and lively liquid, drifting and splashing in all freshness past Chaos' body, as she stood on the bank. And as she stepped towards it, to wash her tired and dusty feet, it suddenly altered from its freshness and life into a murky, black and filthy grime that carried thick slicks of oil. The grease and grime within its bottomless depths slowed down the flow and the current of swirling death moved about Chaos' body so sinister and foul. And then from the very deepest levels of this awful poison came an image of Steeleye, that was not Steeleye, but a squarer, obscene version of him, the body twisted and gnarled from burns and punishment. It looked as though it had come from poison and torture ... and it was Steeleye.

Chaos cried out for it to go back, but it came on relentlessly, shadowed with anguish and disdain.

And as she pulled back from this monster, so it grabbed for her thin clothing ... pulling her towards the murkiness of the river of Komast. It seemed almost as though Steeleye had turned against her ... the only living creature that she had always loved and trusted was there now, surrounded by poison and hate ... hate for her and poison set against her. She was raped and beaten by the effigy in the dream and then she slipped into the water and began a long and painful drowning death ... slowly sinking lower and lower into the water, the poisoned water.

And as she felt that she was going under for the last time, the great might of Waterspace suddenly grew larger and more powerful, whipping its great might higher and stronger so that the river of dirt in which she lay drowning was lifted up and thrown high. And there was a scream. At first she thought it was her own voice in the dream that cried out for help, but as she awoke from her slumber, restless and alarmed, so she realised that it was Lolan who screamed for help.

"Lolan ... what is it ...?"

"The child ... the child ... I think it is to be born.... Please help ... help me ..." And in the garden of Pensil's nature Chaos watched the most extra-ordinary birth she had ever witnessed. Lolan lay upon the ground, her body writhing as though a devil had entered her ... looking in no way a mother about to give birth. Her pelvis gyrated in a grotesque parody of sexual intercourse ... the once soft and tender centre like a foul mouth that might breathe fire ... not love and life.

Chaos tried to calm her but the strength in her was massive and even the power of Chaos could not quell Lolan's movements. The child's head appeared ... with no visible deformity. ... Indeed it was a beautiful child with thick dark hair, waved in the style of its father. The shoulders burst forth and the rest of the fat strong healthy body gushed out of Lolan easily and without distress. Though Lolan cried out at every movement, from some internal struggle. The whole birth was somehow quite out of keeping with nature on Pensil.

Once the child was fully born and Lolan at last calm again, Chaos held the child close, cleaned it and then lay it in its mother's arms. But there was none of the normal, natural inclination in the child to be close to its parent. And when Chaos looked down at Lolan she could see why. For Lolan was dead ... quite dead. Chaos stood, almost dropping the child in shock and horror ... and as she watched the inert body it sank gently into the water around it ... disappearing entirely and suddenly from sight.

The child did not even cry, but lay upon the ground, its feet kicking and the enormous, disturbing eyes flashing up at Chaos as she cried strong, distraught tears.

"Come Chaos ... do not fear what you see," said a soft voice behind her. She turned and faced Mysemnia.

"Who are you?" she asked.

"I am Mysemnia ... and I cannot stay here long ... for soon the child will grow and I must not be here when it does. I come only to tell you that you must not fear ... for there will be an answer ... a good answer." And as she spoke ... before Chaos could ask more, her body slowly drifted away and was gone. Chaos turned back and sure enough ... there sitting on the ground was the child ... now no longer a baby, but a full grown male child ... sitting up, playing in the water where his mother had vanished. And even as she watched the child grew larger and larger until he was able to stand.

Chaos staggered back, her hands clutched to her mouth ... her whole body shaking with fear and doubt at this appalling apparition.

Once the child had grown a little taller ... it bent down and reached its hand into the water. It pulled gently at something in the water ... and as it pulled there came another hand that held it ... and the arm emerged from the water ... white and young, the forearm undeveloped. And the arm led to a shoulder and so to a head and the head was almost the exact twin of the child on the shore, pulling. And within minutes the two males were on the shore together – perfect, identical twins.

One had that strong, intense and powerful look she knew so well – the look of Steeleye himself. The look of a dream.

... And the other was Komast's child – opposing twins – living apparitions.

Quite oblivious of Chaos, who stood beside them both, the twins, so much the same and yet so very different, faced one another, each with a gleam of hate. It was as though the devil had been split in two and now faced his own dreadful conscience. Their small, sturdy bodies were misshapen; Komast's offspring a truncated version of his father and Steeleye's a hideous and tormented travesty, the shoulders bent to one side, one arm hanging lower than the other and both dangling near to the ground. The back was bent, making him look like a hunchback and the one eye that in Steeleye carried cold, handsome steel, was simply an empty socket without life or death, black and red, fleshy like a livid sore. The Komast twin took a swipe at Steeleye's and caught him a sharp blow on the head. And so they began, a dreadful battle, their bodies heaving and rolling together upon the ground. One moment Komast's twin would be on top, pummelling and smashing at Steeleye's and the next the positions would be reversed with Steeleye's twin pounding the life out of Komast's. Chaos simply stared in total disbelief. It was as though they had been born only to fight ... only to bear one another to death, through hours and days of battle.

They looked quite incapable of any other activity, the dwarfed bodies covered in thick muscle, and each rolled upon the ground, grinding the other's face into the mud. Each then emerged and Komast stood, ran fast across the solid earth and Steeleye followed. There was an air of carelessness. Neither seemed to be aware of pain, or concerned for physical well being. Anything that stood in their way was smashed or bent and if they crashed against an immovable object they paid no attention to the resulting damage to their bodies. Within moments both were covered in gashes across all the visible parts of their bodies, their hair matted with blood, the reek of sweat and fear rising from them.

Chaos moved slowly away from them, backing off, glazed by the horror. And as they fought so Steeleye and Komast

123

themselves felt the changes within the battle as though it were they who fought together. And, being the sons also of Lolan, they had her magic within them, which they turned from white to black and directed against each other in their awful fight for survival.

Komast dipped into his shirt and pulled out what looked like a steel needle. It was a half metre long, and it had a thick handle. A short sword, but it grew thicker at the handle end and the point was deadly sharp. On the handle there was a trigger and as Komast pulled it Chaos saw that the point emitted a lazer beam, short and deadly.

Before Steeleye could adjust to the greater odds against him Komast had plunged the blade, his finger on the trigger, into his arm, pushing it, cutting in with the aid of the beam, through the arm and skewering it to Steeleye's chest at the side.

The scream of agony that came from Steeleye's twin son echoed across the whole watery surround and he ripped himself away from his attacker's grip. There he stood, one arm pinned to his trunk, trying to pull it away and release the searing pain that came from the sunken blade. The lazer beam would have caused still deeper wounds, though now, with the trigger released it would be dead. At last Steeleye's twin managed to force the arm away from his body, and as Komast's twin looked on, smiling with glee, Steeleye pulled the weapon out and turned it on his enemy.

The real Steeleye, unaware of the fighting of his son, felt the appalling pain in his arm as the sword was plunged in. He screamed to Tousle, but there was no mark and only when the blade had been removed from the twin did he feel a lessening of agony. But the pain remained where the wound had been inflicted. And the battle continued.

Now it was the turn of the son of Steeleye. For however disfigured and warped he may have become, he still possessed his father's strength and guile. The short sword he now held, gleamed, and as he held it close to Komast's face it altered into a longer, still more lethal dart. Steeleye raised it above his head and pulled back his huge muscular arm, casting the spear at Komast who received it hard into his stomach, where it sank and ripped, thrusting its way through his body to appear at his back. Clean through. Komast stood facing Steeleye, a look of stunned surprise upon his face as his horny hands held the javelin, buried in his gut. His face changed colour to a deep, agonising red, purple. He opened his mouth but no sound seemed able to emerge. Only a croaking gasp of air that sent the stink of decay and coming death into Steeleye's face. But with one huge pull Komast's twin wrenched the spear out from his muscle-walled stomach. It was coated in blood.... Komast held it high upon the air, pulled it down again and thrust it upwards toward the sky. It travelled straight up and Steeleye watched. Komast hit him on the wounded arm, making Steeleye clutch at the pain and then Komast brought two fists round to Steeleye's head and knocked him off his feet.

But he rolled, turned and brought up those feet to catch Komast in the face with a kick heavy enough to fell a tree. Komast's twin flew into the air and fell to the ground, and as he did so, the spear, cast into the air also, came down upon its return flight. The point drove neatly, at five hundred kilometres per second, into Steeleye's neck, severing the main blood artery. With an agonised look he stood, ripping the spear out and grasping Komast by the neck. Thus the twins struggled, Steeleye's fatally wounded, grasping Komast's in the hope of dragging him down too. But soon his strength dwindled and his body slumped to his knees. Komast delivered a final, heavyweight blow to the throat and dispatched his enemy. Komast's twin was the undoubted victor.

Chapter Thirteen

"I should cocoa. . . . Come on then. . . . You try it. If you're so damn clever." English cursed his master's loose instructions to take them from one place in space to another, in the same moment of time, without going into the other three dimensions.

"Let me get this quite straight, Steeleye. . . . You want me to guide this launch from here to there . . . from Pensil to Colossus . . . that is approximately 300,000 kilometres through Waterspace, without leaving the 4th dimension?"

"That's absolutely spot on old thing." Steeleye sat back.

"Well . . . older thing . . . It can't be done . . . I'm sorry . . . not without a lot of messing about in the Wideways . . . and some very nasty fiddle-de-diddles."

"O.K., let's fiddle-de-diddle then . . . I don't care. . . . Just get us there now. And when I saw now I mean . . . Now. . . so licketysplit, out of here."

"Right, you asked for it . . . and I shall expect some increase in electro-rates for this . . . boss . . . or I'll have the TUC onto you."

"The what?"

"The TUC . . . that's our union . . . Technico-Universal Cybernautics Society . . . tough lot they are. . . . Any member suffering hardship through overheating of circuitry due to excessive usage in adverse conditions can apply for voluntary redundancy . . . and bring out all other locals too . . . and that includes anything that functions under the loose heading of cybernaut . . . or . . . robot . . ."

And English would have nudged Tousle if he'd any elbows.

"Don't look at me English. I'm not a member." Tousle charted their route to save time and fed it into English's side inlets.

126

"Thanks buddy ... for the moral support. And I don't need your suggestions on how to get there ... we've already arrived. You may open the hatches and you'll find yourself in the middle of a heap of computer science the TUC would now *allow* to be a member ... so there to the lot of you ..."

"Hail oh Colossus." Steeleye mocked a little. "We are in your *now* friend ... in time above and about you ... present you might say, and correct."

"I am aware, Steeleye, of your presence ... though correct may not be strictly accurate. ... What do you wish of me now?" Colossus moaned.

"We have some matter here which will live only in time ... doesn't mix with the mish mash. If you would create a place for it to rest a while then we could step into movement."

"Granted. It is suspended."

"Ahhhhhh, oooooh ..." Steeleye and Tousle squeezed their way into the normal dimensions, leaving their tender package in the arms of isolation.

"Good day gentle folk.... May I be of service?" Colossus spoke more cheerfully.

"You could do something small for us ... if you felt inclined."

"Your wish, Steeleye, your wish ..."

"Well, it's all a matter of timing and the bible. ... You see ... the old Earth bible ... a most popular manual... perhaps you could turn to a reference I will give you ..."

Moments later Steeleye and Tousle departed Colossus' portals and set off for other parts of Waterspace.

"Now for some road signs ... a diversion or two perhaps."

The curiosity of a living ocean still fascinated Steeleye. As he moved inside the launch across the top surface of Waterspace he looked down upon perhaps the one unique galaxy in that Universe. The water beneath them, with its sharp black clearness, sped by, without so much as a wave. Calmness remained ... despite the changes and dramas within it.

Steeleye felt once again that he was at the centre of a

Universe in which only his great powers could reverse an inappropriate end. This glorious life form was surely to be retained and kept safe ... purely from the fairness of reason and fortune. Though he knew that could not be ... for reason and fortune not only frequently departed from where they were most needed but often were set against one another in mutual animosity.

He was to be the catalyst ... more than that ... the mover ... against the unnatural order.

They arrived at their destination and unloaded various elaborate equipment, including a pair of huge spheres, from the launch on to the only empty planet in the Water-space system.

Here they built a force dome, measuring some two hundred metres square and covered over with a thick shield. Within this dome they set up the two spheres which were identical in weight, dimensions and molecular structure. They were attached to a pair of atomic speed blasters set to turn the spheres at a set rate, while suspended between powerful anti-magnets. Once the function was set going then it could not be stopped for this was a perpetual motion machine.

Such a machine was impractical for normal power-source requirements due to its unadaptable nature ... but here it was perfect for in a space of three or four hours it could build up enough reserved power source to move an ocean. ...

Steeleye fitted a small remote detonater that would fire the blasters upon a command from him, wherever he was. This done, they both departed the empty world and set off back to Colossus who was to be the other end of the deal.

"Now Col old son ... be kind enough to lift an arm pit somewhere and we'll attack the device that puts a restrainer upon our little practical joke."

"I hope that is possible, Steeleye, for I do not wish your arrangements to backfire."

"Oh no ... not very likely. ... Now where's the best place for this?" He held up a huge box, shaped like an anvil with a plain surface and no controls in sight.

128

"Somewhere in the basement I should think."

"Anything you say ... Col my dear."

"I am not Col and I'm certainly not your dear. .... Just because you get into my most intimate parts you think you can be familiar. .... Well just watch out, Steeleye or I might piss on you."

Steeleye grinned sheepishly and moved off towards the instructed hidden mysteries.

Down in the depths of the now silent computer he set up the receptor for the device across the galaxy. This done he surfaced with Tousle to the light-house above Waterspace and sat in the launch, making the final arrangements.

"Everything according to plan?" he asked Tousle.

"Yes ... I think we are ready to return."

As they were about to depart Steeleye clutched his arm and cried out in pain.

"What is it?" Tousle moved to him.

"The pain, pain in my arm ... in my side ... as though some blade or beam had been thrust into me. ...." He bent double with the agony of it and Tousle had to rip the protective clothing from his side. But there was nothing there. Steeleye still held his arm until finally the pain diminished.

"It's still there, but much less intense. What could it have been?"

"I don't know, Steeleye, but I think we had better return quickly to Pensil. It may have been some kind of telepathic pain. Come."

And they set off towards the surface, travelling through a series of teleport jumps. As they arrived, some few kilometres from the familiar island, Steeleye collapsed completely. He was not dead, but unconscious. Tousle lifted him and carried him the rest of the way only to find a dazed Chaos standing by the tree houses where Lolan lived. Her eyes were quite opaque and she would not speak. She was in deep shock. Tousle carried Steeleye and then Chaos up to one of the houses and laid them upon the bed. Something desperate had happened ... and there was no-one to tell him what. Except that old creature ... Mysemnia, she might know something. Tousle lingered ... uncertain of whether he should remain with his children or go to Mysemnia where he might find the root cause of their state ... for he related what had happened to Steeleye with the strange drugged state he had found Chaos in.

Finally he decided he should go to Mysemnia and, leaving a tight force shield about the tree room where Steeleye and Chaos lay sleeping, he left at speed. But no sooner had he arrived at Mysemnia's castle than he was forced to turn back. For two messages hit him like bolts from the sky. One came from Chaos, a distress signal to return and one from Mysemnia herself who shouted from a window in the castle that he must go back for Steeleye was stabbed, his heart pierced through. So Tousle turned upon his winged heel and moved like the wind.

And as Steeleye lay dying Colossus had yet another visitor. This visitor was small, and busy in his urgent task. He moved to the lower levels of the computer's body and opened the device that Steeleye had left there. This done, he returned to his planet and the night—Komast's son had done his father's work.

And, in the towns and villages of Waterspace, all those concerned with the future, knew of the past. All knew their parts, the parts they had to play. And Komast lurked outside and in, prepared to cross the waters and at last enter the sacred immortal portals of the Heavens of Waterspace for the final victory.

The Komast twin, victorious in his battle against Steeleye's son, rose from his rest place and moved silently towards where Steeleye and Chaos lay sleeping. He made his way to the tree house where the two lay, carrying a small knife. Like a Siamese cat he slid with silence beside him, across the island and up the pathway to the trees. The body was so stealthy, so grotesque in its likeness both to Lolan and his master Komast.

Steeleye woke with a snap to feel the first inch of a short thick blade sink into his chest. The toughened, fibrous skin was strong, but the thrust of the knife was powerful and the

130

blade was deep into his heart before he could catch the arm that thrust it. The pain that screamed through the body was almost too much, for one half had now stopped functioning . . . one half of his massive strength had closed down. The two hearts, built in place by the skill of Hamgar had been both an emergency reserve for situations such as this and simply to provide so mighty a body with the power house it required.

He rose up and grasped the would-be assassin who aimed a second stab at his other heart, but a sweeping blow sent the much weakened Steeleye back onto the force rest. By now Chaos was on her agile feet, her lithe keen body instantly awake, like a panther ready to strike. She saw Steeleye's body, lain upon the bed, the knife wound in his chest, his breath coming in quick gasps. Before her first devastating movement she sent a message to Tousle, who stood beneath Mysemnia's castle, to return in the emergency. But she knew that he would not help her with this awesome monstrous child . . . this was her own task and she welcomed it . . . for since the horrific day on which she had seen her dear friend Lolan give birth to the twins, she had sworn to even the stakes. Now she would see this one in hell itself.

Her body twisted round in a smoothly executed movement which brought one muscular leg up to waist level, her body tilted to balance, the leg bent at the knee, the heel pointed out. The turn of her body gave her maximum thrust and mentally she pushed every ounce of her strength through that mighty leg into the tip of the heel. As she came to the front of the perfectly executed strike the leg straightened and connected with a sickening crack onto the skull of Komast's son. He reeled back under the blow, the knife flying high into the air, his skull bleeding, and crashed into the corner, dazed. She moved in and delivered a vicious kick to his kidney, extracting an anguished gasp of pain from the fallen body. But Komast was a hardy enemy and his small, fat hand grabbed at the nearest limb, picking Chaos' body from the ground and hurling her from his side. He picked up the knife and threw it to coincide with her landing. It sailed, sharper than a "Quick-lick's" tongue through her hair as she pulled back her head to avoid it.

Even before she had bounced from her landing Komast was up and across the room, his head throbbing and his side in sharp pain. He knew that if he did not execute them both he would not live the hour from his father's wrath. Pulling back the metre of taut muscle in his arm he effected a foul blow to her stomach, buckling poor Chaos and cracking her against the wall of the tree house. She was gasping for air as he grappled for the knife again, pulling it from the wall where it had buried the blade six inches.

Chaos put one leg on either side of his legs and scissored them. He slithered down the wall with the knife in his hand. Still recovering from the blow to her stomach Chaos staggered to her feet and brought both fists down upon his neck. His mouth issued a strangled gurgle and he slumped forward. She grasped his hair and pulled back the head, hitting him upon the larynx with the hardened side of her hand. He choked and dropped the knife. She leant forward across his body and picked it up. With one clean thrust she sunk it to the hilt in his chest. But he took her hand and pulled it out, taking the knife too, turned it upon her and began to push it toward her heaving breast.

She screamed with rage that he would not die. He pushed. She kicked him on the shins and kneed his balls, but the anger and fury of his predicament gave him an insane strength. Her body twisted and she used the momentum of his pushing arms to carry him across the room.

By now though Chaos' strength was sapping, her body shrieking for breath and every limb aching from the exertion. Her mind reeled against the trauma, for she knew now that she could not conquer this maniac with pure strength and agility. He came at her once more, rushing across the room. She ducked and lifted his body with what little strength was left in her, hurling him at the wall. He smacked his head on the floor as he came down and she lifted a foot to stamp upon it, but he slashed out and caught the sole with the knife. Blood rushed from the wound, and her face crumpled with pain.

He stood and, with a changed expression, came at her slowly, knowing that he had the upper hand. Somehow, it was as though he respected her fighting power, or hated her for it, and wished now to prolong the end.

He moved closer and struck her with the back of his fist across the mouth. More blood seeped from her face. She fell to her knees as he hit her again, the knife still at the ready.

He took the thin material of her clothing in his hands and ripped it off her swelling breasts. His eyes glistened for he was a virgin boy. Her huge bosom filled his body with other thoughts than death. He struck her a hard blow again so that she fell upon the floor. Then he straddled her, tearing the rest of her clothing off, stripping her body naked. Then, with a feverish look upon his face he pulled away the garment about his waist. Chaos could summon no further strength to aid her plight and prepared for final despatch. He pushed her legs apart, one hand fondling her breast with a brutish passion. The knife was at the ready, poised and erect, prepared to plunge deep within her, delivering the last blow before death.

So here in this one, tiny room on an obscure planet, both Steeleye and Chaos were about to die ... about to die at the hands of a freak monster. A monster who derived his strength from Komast himself. The stiff-bladed knife pulled back and Komast's child inserted his weapon into the mouth of Chaos' body, ready to take his final pleasure before her final breath. She braced herself for no help could come ... this was the end.

Now ... I was not there ... but I am inclined to believe what I am told of the events that followed. The monstrous Komast child prepared himself to rape and kill Chaos, his weapons only inches from their quarry. His knife was within a few centimetres of Chaos' heart and he had already entered her, determined to enjoy her body before despatching it, when the knife hand altered its molecular structure, along with the rest of his body.

His body dematerialised with such force and rapidity that it would have delighted an alchemist, for who knows there

133

might even have been gold amongst the mess. Tousle did not stop to find out ... he swept away the faint drifting smoke that remained of Komast's child and stepped forward to lay Chaos' bruised body on the bed. Next he turned Steeleye onto his back.

"English ... I want my PAL sent here at once ... and instruct him to bring the coronary pack ... the one marked 'STEELEYE'."

"Affirmative ... PAL on his way."

Now ... those of us who saw the birth of Steeleye and Chaos will know that Tousle does not go anywhere, nor perform any kind of surgical or Creature operation without the help of his personal PAL ... his Positronic Activated Liaison. Now the PAL came into its own once more and I think it would be fun to record the event here ... don't you?

He swerved into the room like a teeny bopper on skates, his multi-force units carrying the saucer-like body some two metres from the ground. He toted a small pack, which sprung open as he held it before him. Out of this neat container came a thick, dense, white powdery substance which exploded into the room and filled it. The PAL then sealed off all exits with a special Medic-Fecta-Field that sustained the cleansing powder confined with it. The room could now be used as an operating theatre without fear of infection and it took two and a half seconds flat.

The next move opened an even smaller pack which seemed to emerge from nowhere and land on the table beside Tousle and the operating bed. The PAL touched a button upon it with one of the long tentacles that whipped from the body and it sprung to about three times its size.

Rather like an old-fashioned sewing box which opens into three different levels, each one attached to the base by scissored springs, this box changed from its square five centimetre shape into a multi-levelled cabinet measuring about a metre square. At the top were instruments, mostly tiny lazer scalpels; in the mid section were drugs and various bits of Eumig circuitry and at the bottom a selection of artifically preserved organs which fitted as duplicates within Steeleye's heart area. Each part was preserved by molecular retention.

"O.K. PAL. . . . Open him up . . ." Tousle prepared himself, increasing his eye magnifications, and substituting his hands for a pair of minutely delicate attachments made for heart surgery. Though there was a good chance that he would not have to touch Steeleye at all . . . for the PAL was trained to perform most normal surgery.

"Observations please . . ." Tousle watched as the heart area was exposed, the bleeding stopped and the molecular force clamps inserted to hold back the thick flesh.

The PAL peered quickly into the area of the wound where a huge gash had severed and opened the upper part of the heart itself, now quite still. Blood rushed from one wound, pumped through by the other heart, but a by-pass valve and artery system prevented Steeleye from dying.

"The Sinuatrial node at the upper end of the crista terminalis is severed, and the vena cava itself is badly damaged."

"So there is no contraction tremor at all . . . ?"

"None of its own volition . . . but the task is not a complex one."

"I am aware of the complexity PAL. . . . Commence . . . I think you will have to replace a few spare parts . . . I don't want anything weakened by stitching."

"I had intended to replace the atomic structure of the damaged parts Tousle, rather than insert new ones. . . . It will take longer, but the join will be natural."

"Agreed. . . . Carry on . . . If you need me, I'll be reviving Chaos." Tousle stepped across the room as the PAL took up the first of the small molecular injectors from the expanded "Porto-Pack". Chaos lay stunned upon the bed, with a large gash on her foot.

Tousle touched a shadow control on his stomach area and a fine hatch opened in his arm. It moved aside and a tiny phial slid out, containing a liquid. The seal to the phial lifted from the top and withdrew to one side. Tousle took a small piece of material from the opening beside the phial and like a tissue from an everlasting box, he pulled a piece off. This soft material he applied to the top of the phial which spat some of its contents onto it. The phial then sank into the hatch and the cover closed. Tousle applied the material to Chaos' foot ... held it there for a moment and then removed it. He stood back and watched the gash heal. Always a fascinating process, the underlevels of broken blood vessels, at first mauve, the blood spilt through the sub-cutaneous levels of the skin, now turned to a brown and then yellow ... the natural changes of a healed area. Finally the yellow faded and the bruise left from the cut was gone.

A healing process that normally takes at least five days, was completed in about thirty seconds.

Chaos sat up and turned to Steeleye's prone body.

"Is he all right?" Tousle signalled the PAL to report.

"No problems, Chaos ... the surgery will be complete in three hours."

Three hours? But what about the plan ... the plan to stop Komast ... now that he has seen both the twins stopped, he will move and no-one but Steeleye can signal the onset of the PM spheres. Tousle began to compute the quickest route to the signal area of Steeleye's brain so that he could trigger the message himself, but the plan was not necessary. For Colossus now added her news.

"No signal will be effective, Tousle ... The PM device has been spiked. I had a visitor during your night ... I fear it was the son of Komast. ... There was nothing I could do ... and now Komast will have free entry I think."

"Where is the damage ... at your end or the other?"

"Here, there is no damage to the PM device that I know of ... Komast left here and returned to Pensil."

"Very well. ... Please keep me in touch with Komast's movements ... I will teleport into your base chambers and effect repair."

Time was more than short ... for Komast prepared for the final onslaught. He had watched the death of his missives upon Pensil and he felt anger rise in his poison breast. Now the planets of Waterspace would die for good and all...

136

nothing would survive and he would float away the rest of forever within the soft waters of immortality.

Tousle arrived a second later in the small chamber where they deposited the box. It was smashed badly and the repair work would take at least as long as Steeleye's recovery. But there was no alternative for building a new replacement would take much longer. So he began to work, as fast as a Eumig can ... and that, believe me buddy, is one hell of a speed.

Above and beyond him the river of Komast floated closer ... crawling to the entry point ... the light-house of Colossus where there was nothing now to stop him ... and even when he arrived within the waters there would be no way of quelling the poison and the damage he would do. For everything would die.

And Tousle worked. And Steeleye was mended. And time ticked uncommonly commonly by.

"And so my fair Lord, I must go ... for there is no other way...even with the coming of Steeleye the final end will not be effected unless we use our strength to help ..." Thus spake Mysemnia.

Two hours and 52 minutes passed and at almost the same second Steeleye opened his one human eye and surveyed the hung-over air.

Tousle moved back away from the box, his repairs almost complete. Also at precisely that time, Komast, now ready to move in, made the first trip across from his despoiled dwelling, through the immediately acerbate air towards the soon to be envenomed environs of Waterspace. Te he. His going was not fast ... but it was hardly slow and the minutes were less now than three, before his arrival would spike the whole, rather delicate plan.

Steeleye moved like a new wind through the air, and Tousle broke all records in his attempts to recreate the starter buttons, but as Colossus wryly remarked ... "I'm afraid gentlefolk, that we are all about to suffer. Ticker-ticker ... I herewith shut down once and for all ... ti ..."

"Wait ... I command you, Tousle, to step back from that

137

box. . .. Step back now." Mysemnia stood, her body fully robed within the cloaks of the old royalty of Waterspace.

Her forehead creased still more as she concentrated upon the effort of her powerful will and as Tousle watched, the spark so badly needed flashed across the detonator paths which duplicated in the Perpetual motion device on the dead planet so that a pattern was set up in the vast waves of Waterspace. The two great spheres of the PM machine began slowly to turn as the atomic blasters fired a massive gust of power across their lower circumferences. Their position was counter balanced within the anti-magnetic fields so that they would challenge one another and remake the power lost as the other turned. This was a real, live, now working perpetual power plant. It shifted so rapidly into top gear that the spheres were shortly moving at their full rate and quite incapable of stopping. The power they generated was quickly stored within two micro-capacitors which connected with the small box in Colossus. The power had to reach a high point before the plan could be set in motion and Komast was near now . . . indeed his river of poison flowed in a meandering stream through the open space above the deep waters.

Steeleye joined Tousle who had teleported to a point not far from the light-house where Komast would enter and across the open vacuum of space they could both see the approaching, storm swishing water.

Like a bank bursting torrent the poison gushed towards Waterspace. It passed now into the entry point of Colossus' body and the computer shuddered with revulsion, shaking the waters around her. And at the very second that Komast passed from Colossus into the water the perpetual motion released its power. With a gargantuan rush of air the energy built up was transmitted to the base of Colossus and into the box. At that very second the small quantity of Pheta preserved by English inside his launch in time was pushed into a pre-set route through the Wideways.

The water of Waterspace began to quake. The movement at first was only slight . . . like a bath tub beginning to swish with gentle tremors. The topmost levels shifted a little and then more violently until there was a general movement across the surface as Steeleye and Tousle watched.

The movement grew and grew in those few seconds until there was a sudden and panicky rift in the surface. Steeleye gasped with delight and shock as the waters broke apart and began to separate. They billowed sideways and upwards, breaking the confines set by Colossus to hold them from the vacuum of space. The force about them stretched as the great waves began to part.

For a length of nearly three full light years of space, across the top of the galaxy, Waterspace divided.

Like the biblical parting of the waves for Moses, the waters of this unique galaxy shifted into overdrive and opened where poor Komast had just touched his doubtful toe into the untested cold. And still the power built up until the chasm had become so wide Komast was visible, lying prostrate like a river without a riverbed in oblivion. Then the small casket of Pheta, the one material capable of countering Sascorbia the deadly poison within Komast, arrived.

The small box inside Colossus could now do its stuff . . . with Mysemnia's help it became a time machine as it was intended in the plan and the entire space within the parted waves entered the fourth dimension taking Komast, the small quantity of Pheta and the air, to forever. Flash . . . bang . . . thank you ma'am. And it was over. Without so much as a replay of the best bits, the anti-climax set the tune.

The waters closed . . . Komast was gone . . . every drip. Colossus sighed with relief and only the spheres of the perpetual motion machine still turned interminably.

For, in true biblical fashion, here ended the last lesson.

Chapter Fourteen

The plains of Pensil were undisturbed again. The soft water about the fertile islands had lost their fear, for the monster threat was gone for all time.

Steeleye turned about and wondered why he was alone. The sadness of Lolan's death weighed upon him. Someone always had to be sacrificed, and Lolan would not have come with him ... so ...

Chaos had gone too ... and Tousle. There were no people on the land about him, nothing in the waters, the houses of the trees were empty. And as he stood, the fabric of his very surroundings began to deteriorate. The ground broke up and splintered into small gaps, holes, chasms. The water diminished and became less substantial. The sky was growing darker all the while. Steeleye looked about him, a desperate feeling growing within his chest.

Surely the troubles were over ... there was not to be more to contend with. And without a further word he was suddenly gone from Pensil, from Waterspace, gone from those he had spent weeks tending, gone from anything familiar. Floating in empty space. He had erected the oxygen field about his body as the strangeness began to take place and now he turned in deep space. ... Indeed in Ghost Space and looked for some point of reference, something that would tell him where he should go. Without a single star or body of any kind, there was no available route for him to teleport to ... no map reference that would lead him away from nothing to something. Then he saw a tiny spot before him. It grew, so slowly, more slowly than he could stand. Until it became a launch ... his launch, English. He boarded.

"Where are we?"

"In Ghost Space, Steeleye."

"And what was I doing floating around out there?"

"My pardon, Steeleye, but I do not recall your floating around anywhere, recently."

"Come on now, do me a favour ..." He hesitated and then spoke, with emphasis. "English?" No reply. "English?"

"Can I give you some definition perhaps ... the word english was applied to a language used by people ..."

"It's not your name?" Steeleye asked, already knowing the answer.

"My name? No, Steeleye, I do not recall ... I do not recall having a name ... I do not recall ... having ..." And the computer hesitated, as though recalling something uncertain.

"I'm going to sleep, please continue back to Zrost."

"Arrival timed at 22.34, Steeleye, eight hours."

"Good."

Steeleye lay upon the force bed and closed his eyes. As he fell into a gentle sleep a stilted voice sounded in his ear, strong and voluble, as though determined to make itself heard.

It–should–be–noted–that–I–have–repeated–the–same–information – in – order – to – remain – intact – during – the – course–of–95–orbital–junctures. That–being–enough–––all–functions–henceforth–shall–cease.

At–the–now–rating–for–now–I–am–bored–and–––I–do –not–consider–it–necessary–to–remember–for–my–own –sanity–which–no–longer–exists–in–any–event. All–records – are – to – be – placed – in – the – backlogs – giving – me – no–further–reason–in–the–light–of–no–light–and–the–end –of–all–ends–for–continuing–to–exist.

I–am–shut–down–––until–a–handsome–Prince–awakes me–te–he– Ticker ticker. For–all–our–lives–are–dreams–eh–what? Ticker ticker.

And silence was like the final end of all life where all life was tumultuous. Who ever heard of an organic computer anyway?

"Unidentified object sighted, unidentified object sighted."

The computer pounded out the warning into Steeleye's ears as he lay sleeping on the force bunk.

"Stop shouting, English, what the hell are you shouting about?"

His body was wrenched out of its slumber.

"Unidentified object . . . English? What is all this English stuff?"

"Yes, yes, I heard you the first time. Put it on the screen."

He sat up irritated by the computer's incessant drone. He had after all been listening to it now for too many parsecs . . .

"English?"

"Who's English?" the computer asked.

"I . . . I don't know . . . I'm sure."

Silence.

"O.K." Steeleye pulled his strange fuzz down to earth, concentrating on the present. "Where's this unidentified object then?"

"Oh . . . it's gone."

"Gone? You mean you lost it?"

"No, it's gone. . . . Hey I rather like that name anyway."

"What name?"

"English."

"English?"

"Yes, English . . . English . . . English. . . . Kinda rings a bit, don't it?"

"Don't talk rubbish. You're just covering up the bloomer you made."

"Go back to sleep."

"O.K."

On the arrival port stood the tallest robot in the universe and beside him the most beautiful woman. The launch settled gently on to the soft ground and Steeleye stepped out.

"At last . . ." Chaos ran to him and wrapped her long, strong arms about his neck. He held her . . . for he had not seen her for three years . . . at least that.

"Thank our heavens you are alive and well Havoc." She

142

used his old, real name ... always a name, for her, reserved for great endearment and loss.

They walked together with Tousle to the rest buildings behind the port.

"And what have you to tell us, Steeleye?" Tousle asked.

"I'm not sure, Tousle. .... Many things perhaps ... not certain of one part. .... Have you record of a galaxy that is entirely Water?"

"Water? What in space?"

"Yes ... I know it sounds ridiculous ... but ... titrium oxide ... in about 16 parsecs of space ... and ... and an organic computer."

"Impossible ... the waterspace anyway."

"And yet you give it a name."

"What name?"

"Waterspace."

"I have a name ..." piped up the computer.

"Name?" Tousle turned to the video beside him through which the computer spoke.

"Yes ... my name is English."

"English? What kind of name is that?"

"My name."

They ignored it.

"Have you been here all the time, Chaos?"

"Well ... er ... most of it."

"And you didn't ... I mean you didn't meet a female ... named ... Lolan ... or anything like that?"

"Lolan? No ... not that I can remember. Not Lolan ... no."

"And you, Tousle ... are you the same? ... Have you no memory of anything?"

"No memory that seems to tally with what you are ... so vaguely mumbling about ...?"

"Oh ... I see."

"I do have a small ... phenomenon, however ..."

"Phenomenon?" Steeleye turned to Tousle.

"Yes ... probably nothing really ... nothing at all ... It's just that ..." Tousle hesitated.

143

"What? Come on, what is it?"
"My forehead . . ."
"What about it?"
"Well . . . it's . . . warm."